# The Dark Wings of the Stage

*A seasoned playwright embarks on her most challenging work, the script for a play she thinks will never be staged, because of its unflinching look at the pain she endured in a past relationship. She is assisted by a mature male student who has chosen to study her work and methods. Sometimes encouraging, at other times highly critical, he ultimately becomes crucial to the script's completion.*

## Also by Pearl Watkins

*The Reluctant Chameleon*

*The Stability of Everyday Objects*

*Go*

*Thin Ice*

# The Dark Wings of the Stage

**Pearl Watkins**

© 2023 by Pearl Watkins

ISBN 979-8-218-32149-9

First edition book and cover layouts by Maggie Powell Designs
www.maggiepowelldesigns.com

Printed in the United States of America

All rights reserved. No part of this publication may be reproduced,
distributed, or transmitted in any form or by any means, including
photocopying, recording, or other electronic or mechanical methods,
without the prior written permission of the publisher.

*She left him standing there in a melancholic frenzy, and closing the door collapsed against it, blazing and quivering. This is how an actress reaches the dark wings of the stage, after running through the emotions of a lifetime in a hundred and twenty minutes.*

**Opium Fogs**
Rosemary Tonks

*"All the world's a stage..."*

**As You Like It**
W.S.

# The Dark Wings
# of the Stage

# OVERTURE

LANA      A black hole. Yes, call it that. A black hole into which are flung: a man, a woman, miles and miles of open road, a bed, a sigh, a red towel, a train journey, the unbuttoned cuff of a white shirt – ah, there it is, the first pain – no, not pain itself, rather the memory of pain, which is different, no?

TOMOS      How d'you mean, different?

LANA      Because the act of remembering is interposed like a layer of protective gauze between the heart and the hurt. ...Heart....heat....hurt....hut – how controlled we are by the letters of the alphabet.

TOMOS      Stay on the subject.

LANA      Oh, 'scusi. Where was I? Ah yes, pain. Pain can only be immediate, felt when felt. Remembered pain or – more accurately – the pain felt when remembering, is simply nostalgia, a faint, generalised ache, that longing for the past (with all its pains) that the Welsh understand so well they have a word for it: *hiraeth*.....here-aye-th, with the final two consonants as at the conclusion of 'teeth' and not as at the beginning of the definite article, a small but crucial distinction.

TOMOS      You're drifting off the subject again.

LANA      I'm just getting myself in the mood. I'll probably throw these first pages away. That's what you're supposed to do, isn't it? Where was I?

TOMOS      Flinging–

— 1 —

LANA     Ah yes, flinging items into the black hole:
         wanderlust of him and her–

TOMOS    Who?

LANA     Our antagonists.

TOMOS    Don't you mean protagonists?

LANA     Do I?

TOMOS    I see. You may want to consider resisting the
         temptation to be – original.

LANA     Seems to me I must resist the temptation to be
         unoriginal. I resume: wanderlust (her and him),
         lack of motivation (her), rage (him), the urge
         to please (her), the desire to control (him), the
         stubborn struggle against mortality (him and her),
         the urge to copulate (him)–

TOMOS    Steady on.

LANA     Ah yes. This is only the overture after all. The
         music must swell, yes, but only sufficiently to – to
         intrigue and not satisfy. I must merely – hint?

TOMOS    You don't want to overwhelm them right at the
         beginning.

LANA     Yes, you're right, satisfaction must come later,
         you're right, you're right. ...Which do you like
         better, by the way – rage or anger?

TOMOS    In this context?

LANA     Obviously.

TOMOS   Anger. No – rage. Mm – no – anger. On a purely
        syllabic basis.

LANA    ...?

TOMOS   Anger.

LANA    I agree. Anger then. No, it's not – strong enough.
        It has to be rage.

TOMOS   Why did you bother asking me?

LANA    You helped me eliminate the unwanted. So what
        have we got? Wanderlust (her and him), lack of
        motivation (her), rage (him), the urge to please
        (her), the desire to control (him), the stubborn
        struggle against mortality (him and her), the urge
        to– Did I say wheels? Did I fling wheels in?

TOMOS   No.

LANA    Definitely wheels. Also–

TOMOS   How about a few specifics?

LANA    A few....?

TOMOS   Details. For the texture.

LANA    A few trivialities....for the texture... Good idea.
        Him: a straw hat with a dark green band worn
        absolutely horizontal. Intentionally, deliberately,
        calculatedly.

TOMOS   Careful with those adverbs. And what do you
        mean, calculatedly?

LANA    The usual. To attract the opposite sex.

— 3 —

TOMOS   Okay. Go on.

LANA    Perhaps one adverb would suffice....deliberately, I'll use that one. A straw hat worn deliberately horizontal. A flared, calf-length, wrapover cotton skirt–

TOMOS   This is still him?

LANA    Of course not. Obviously not.

TOMOS   You never know.

LANA    When was the last time you saw a man in a skirt – and I don't mean a kilt.

TOMOS   Yesterday.

LANA    Yesterday?! You're kidding.

TOMOS   Forget it.

LANA    Her: a flared skirt made of a thin printed cotton, manufactured and utilised all over the Indian subcontinent, also exported to other countries including the United Kingdom, and a staple of the seventies bedsit, background colour indigo with an orange border so that the chain of bright blue elephants–

TOMOS   Blue elephants? Now who's kidding.

LANA    I most certainly am not. There's power in authenticity. Anyway, it's only cloth. And the elephants' ears are small because the garment was made in India. For heaven's sake, it's only a design on cloth.

— 4 —

TOMOS   Whatever you say.

LANA    You asked for details. Into the black hole with them, those blue elephants with their small ears, and after them a smile, a parting, a long tearful train journey then–

TOMOS   –You already said that.

LANA    What?

TOMOS   Train journey.

LANA    Is it confusing?

TOMOS   How many train journeys were there?

LANA    One. The whole thing is one long journey but there is only one train journey.

TOMOS   Mmm....okay. So what were the other modes of transport?

LANA    Other modes of transport, that's very – formal. You don't look like the formal type.

TOMOS   What should I say then?

LANA    No, really it's fine. The other main mode of transport is Greyhounds.

TOMOS   The dog?

LANA    The bus.

TOMOS   Oh, right, okay.

LANA    So what do you think so far? Be honest, I can take it.

— 5 —

TOMOS  I think you're off to a good start. But may I
mention something?

LANA  Of course. You know I want your input.

TOMOS  Don't confuse authenticity with catharsis.

LANA  As if I would. So you – you really like it?

TOMOS  I do.

LANA  Whooppee. End of overture, yes?

TOMOS  Yeah.

*END OF OVERTURE*

TOMOS   The black hole, it's a metaphor, right? A symbol.

LANA    Yes.

TOMOS   For?

LANA    The black hole is....let's say it represents humanity's appetite for romance.

TOMOS   Woh.

LANA    Let us also say that the sky is white, the scenery–

TOMOS   Is this the first scene now?

LANA    Scene one, yes.

TOMOS   And the curtains?

LANA    Curtains?

TOMOS   I think you should observe all the proper conventions.

LANA    Conventions? But I'm rearing to go!

TOMOS   Just saying...

LANA    You're right, you're right. Tedious, but necessary. Theatrical conventions, you mean. Never neglect the little things. Very well. The overture to act one has concluded, the applause subsides–

TOMOS   You hope.

LANA    What did you say?

TOMOS   Nothing. Go on.

— 7 —

LANA    A crescendo of applause....which subsides as the curtains open and act one begins. Scene one – are you with me?

TOMOS   Yes. Act one, scene one. Proceed.

ACT ONE

# ACT ONE, SCENE ONE

LANA    Okay, here goes. The sky is white with cloud, the
        scenery frosted with a light covering of snow, the
        conifers innumerable and, in the background, the
        four iconic faces, colossal, unsmiling, carved into
        the pale grey stone of the mountain's chilled hip,
        instantly recognisable.

TOMOS   That's very poetic.

LANA    Thank you.

TOMOS   Not sure where we are... would it kill you to
        explain?

LANA    Yes, it would, just at this moment. Our two
        antagonists – no, I refuse to change it – our
        antagonists are about to enter. They are tourists
        and this is a tourist destination. The gods have
        proved very good location scouts. But what is that
        in the upstage left corner of the stage? Okay, that's
        scene one.

*END OF ACT ONE, SCENE ONE*

— 9 —

TOMOS   That's it? It's very short.

LANA   I've seen shorter.

TOMOS   Yeah, well, in movies but this isn't a movie. Is it?

LANA   Perhaps. Who knows?

TOMOS   No harm in fantasising, I suppose. So what is it in the corner of the stage?

LANA   A bed.

TOMOS   Ah.

LANA   I knew you'd like that.

TOMOS   But no characters. No beings.

LANA   No, but we have the promise of....which euphemism shall I use?

TOMOS   What are you talking about?

LANA   If it were possible to measure such a phenomenon, if someone bothered to conduct such an experiment – but perhaps they have! – I suspect it would be observed that some specific physiological and psychological changes would be seen to take place in a human being when they anticipate the opportunity of watching moments of intimacy between other human beings, don't you agree?

TOMOS   I'm still trying to understand the question.

LANA   I'm not saying these changes are necessarily positive, by which I mean they may not in themselves elicit pleasure. In fact the opposite

— 10 —

may well be the case, meaning a negative reaction occurs and no pleasure is elicited; so that, in this instance, the observation of the activities becomes merely an exercise in reinforcing an already established negative opinion, perhaps based on a lack of pleasure, in one's own experiences that is, of what is being observed – a kind of masochistic notetaking, if you like...

TOMOS I'm not following this.

LANA However I am convinced that basically we are all like Chance the Gardener – we like to watch.

TOMOS I have no idea what you're talking about.

LANA Never mind. We shall not agree about everything.

TOMOS I hate to say it but I may have bitten off more than I can–

LANA No, please! Stay.

TOMOS If this is the way you mean to go on, I may not be able to stand it.

LANA I shall try to do better.

TOMOS Okay.

LANA And you in turn must learn to be a little more – accommodating and patient. Scene two. Are you with me?

TOMOS Yes, yes. Scene two.

LANA Good.

— 11 —

TOMOS   I think I'm being very accommodating – and
         patient. Just stay on course and be clear, okay? Or
         I'm off.

LANA    I shall be the very embodiment of concision and
         pith. Why are you smiling?

TOMOS   I wasn't. Go on.

LANA    Scene two. A plain room. It is evening. Yes, you
         were, you were smiling.

TOMOS   Forget it. But the curtains didn't close.

LANA    Who cares!

TOMOS   The audience! Have a heart!

LANA    Yes, yes, of course. The audience, how stupid of
         me. They too must be pressed to the edge of the
         black hole–

TOMOS   Do black holes have edges?

LANA    No, they have event horizons. Don't interrupt –
         where was I? – pressed to the edge of the black
         hole without their realising it. But how are they
         to be led by the nose if a ring is not first inserted?
         No, I don't like that, wrong animal. I need some
         creature more....more easily intimidated, can't
         think of one at present....they must first be – be
         – coralled like – like nervous sheep, yes, that's
         it, sheep, and the sheepdog, making no physical
         contact with them, yet anticipating and quelling
         any frisson of mutiny or distraction, urges them
         in the desired direction where, confused but

— 12 —

controlled, they all, of their own volition bodily
hurl themselves in.

TOMOS  But what's the ring? What's the inducement?

LANA  Anticipation! The bed is still in position!

TOMOS  Are you sure that's enough? What about a few
more details?

LANA  Oh this is impossible. All right, all right. I'll
provide them very soon. I'm ready to go on to
scene two now, do you mind?

TOMOS  Yes – I mean, no. Just go ahead.

LANA  Forget the curtain – we'll do it with lights.

## ACT ONE, SCENE TWO

LANA    A plain boarding-house room in the northern hemisphere. The bed is still in position. It is evening. In the room are two bodies of unequal stature, both unclothed. She is the shorter but he is the thinner. They are vertical. He bends towards her smiling – no – *beaming*: she is the earth and he is the sun, shining down upon her. She raises her face to the warmth. On her he is bestowing light and heat, the light and heat of his adoration and desire for sex – ah! – such anticipation, such energy....and such agony to recall...

TOMOS    Don't get distracted.

LANA    Easy for you to say. Where was I? Light....heat.... yes. The female is shy but ravishing as befits a liebhaberin–

TOMOS    A what?

LANA    Liebhaberin.

TOMOS    And what's that?

LANA    It's a German word.

TOMOS    I don't care if it's Hindustani, it's showing off, that's what it is.

LANA    Isn't it obvious from the context what it means?

TOMOS    No. Look, do you have to?

LANA    Yes, actually.

— 14 —

TOMOS   Then you have to translate it, you have to translate
        it. Or the audience will have no idea what you're
        talking about.

LANA    I thought it might separate the wheat from the
        chaff.

TOMOS   It will separate the German-speaker from the non-
        German-speaker, that is what it will do and that is
        *all* it will do.

LANA    Eliot didn't translate. Why did you say that twice
        by the way?

TOMOS   What?

LANA    That I have to translate it.

TOMOS   I don't know. I suppose I was being – emphatic.
        Eliot who?

LANA    TS. It's your way of keeping me on the straight and
        narrow, isn't it?

TOMOS   Oh please.

LANA    Well, you'll be glad to hear that you succeeded.

TOMOS   Good. *Translate it.*

LANA    Liebhaberin – leading lady. Satisfied? Right,
        where was I? So – is it shocking that our shy but
        ravishing....um...

TOMOS   Leebthingy–

LANA    –*leading lady* is about to give herself to an
        improbable leading man – a leading man without–

— 15 —

TOMOS  So what's the German for leading ma–

LANA  –Don't interrupt!

TOMOS  Well, excuse me!

LANA  – where was I? – give herself, give herself to – to
a leading man – leading man – to a leading man
without the usual leading man qualities?

TOMOS  And what are they?

LANA  Mm? Oh – the usual, good looks, broad shoulders,
long legs, as if you couldn't guess.

TOMOS  And he doesn't have these.

LANA  Nope.

TOMOS  It's a tragedy then?

LANA  How should I know? I just make this stuff up as I
go along.

TOMOS  You expect me to believe that?

LANA  These stories usually are – tragic.

TOMOS  So what's leading man in German?

LANA  Liebhaber.

TOMOS  Leap harbour? Weird.

LANA  Oh, this is impossible. How am I to sustain a
thought if you keep interrupting? Just look at how
long it's taken me to express that one idea! Will
you please let me get to the end of something?

— 16 —

TOMOS   Go ahead. I won't say a word.

LANA     Sanctimonious pig.

TOMOS   What was that?

LANA     Nothing. Just a quote. Where-was-I?

TOMOS   In a room with two bodies of unequal stature.

LANA     Ah yes. A room, two bodies, unequal stature,
         unclothed, vertical, she shorter he thinner....he
         bends towards her beaming, she the earth and
         he the sun, shining upon her. She raises her face
         to the warmth. He is bestowing on her his light
         and warmth, the light and warmth of his sexual
         craving. The female is shy but ravishing as befits a
         liebhaberin so is it shocking that our leading lady
         is about to give herself to a frankly scrawny male
         – a leading man without leading-man qualities? ...
         Thank you.

TOMOS   Don't mention it. Does he have an erection?

LANA     What do you think?

TOMOS   Just asking. Please continue.

LANA     It will eventually become fairly clear to even the
         most impartial outside observer that–

TOMOS   You're waffling.

LANA     Oops. I was. It is clear that while she is reduced
         by uncertainty – no, that's no good....what's the
         word I'm looking for...

TOMOS   Insecurity?

— 17 —

LANA      Nnnn-ot quite...

TOMOS   A need to please?

LANA      Better...

TOMOS   Nonchalance?

LANA      Possibly...

TOMOS   Deficiencies in upbringing?

LANA      Goes without saying...

TOMOS   What then?

LANA      I've got it. Her tender heart.

TOMOS   That should get a few gasps from the audience.

LANA      Let me finish. It is clear that while she is reduced
          by her tender heart, he is raised up by his extreme
          desire (which he disguises as sincerity) and by his
          success at extracting her from her clothing. That's
          it.

TOMOS   Raised up? May I suggest a glance at one's
          Thesaurus?

LANA      One's? Oh I see now, you become formal when
          you want to admonish. They'll know what I mean.
          But wait – the romance.

TOMOS   Oh good, at last.

LANA      Are you being sarcastic?

TOMOS   No!

— 18 —

LANA    All right, all right. Here goes. Dozens of small
        children rush on from all directions–

TOMOS   All?

LANA    Yes.

TOMOS   Even from within the audience?

LANA    Yes – *no!* – I don't care. They can be flown on
        wires, for all I care. Where was I? – a dozen small
        children rush on with thick white unlit candles
        almost as tall as themselves, about three feet.
        Small for a human being but tall for a candle.
        The children come to a halt on stage, randomly
        positioned. They place their candles carefully
        upright in front of themselves and pause for a
        moment before each takes from a pocket a box of
        matches which he – they are all boys – which he
        holds to show the audience. They shake the boxes
        briefly, creating a moment of tuneless percussive
        music. Then each extracts one match, strikes it and
        in unison they apply their burning matches to the
        wicks of the candles whereupon the candle flames
        flare up – flare up as high, plump and glowing as
        his erection.

TOMOS   I love it!

LANA    There are men so accustomed to the clenched
        hand that the cunt is a disappointment. This is
        not one. There are men who know how to caress a
        woman to a climax. This is not one. There are men
        whose drive to fill a woman's hole has displaced
        their desperation to plug another hole – that

— 19 —

which gapes within their own psyches, causing inextinguishable pain. For these men, sex is religion. This is one.

TOMOS  Go on, this is terrific.

LANA  The upper reaches of the body, that's where her interest lies, the mouth, the lips, the tongue, the breath, passion as expressed facially.

TOMOS  Yeah, women like that stuff.

LANA  Here he is utterly lacking. He has opened his mouth, prized open her mouth, stuck his tongue in and now he's ready to go on to the – the meatier bits. Those areas that interest her – and would do so much to arouse her – they remain neglected, unattended to, they languish.

TOMOS  That is sad.

LANA  Quite. Complete absence of foreplay then. He heads straight for the high altar. After the initial burblings that pass for reverence, there are three main attractions: two are round and more or less identical and one is roughly triangular and surprising in the abundance of its hirsute covering and its range of colouring: black, blond, brown, auburn, even white – why not? – the young do not have a monopoly on this activity even if – with the stunning arrogance of youth – they are incapable of imagining a pair of ancients disrobing and happily screwing. This triangle is light brown.

TOMOS  Is that what I think it is?

— 20 —

LANA     Yes. Let the fucking go on, but for no longer than
         it does in reality when two inflamed strangers fuck
         for the first time. Correction: one is inflamed, the
         other waits to be ignited (and will be left waiting).
         Eleven thrusts then, which is still ten more than
         she needs to discover that he is typical of his
         species: he can fill the hole without causing the
         least disturbance in any other part of her anatomy
         – unless you count pity as a disturbance.

TOMOS    My god, that's cynical.

LANA     I am putting into words what is usually left unsaid.
         This can be upsetting.

TOMOS    Nevertheless...

LANA     Clarity is sometimes the most difficult thing to
         accept – the absence of veils.

TOMOS    I'm fine with it, I'm just thinking of the audience.

LANA     Oh, screw the audience.

TOMOS    How many thrusts?

LANA     One.

TOMOS    Ha-ha-ha! Glad to see you still have your sense of
         humour.

LANA     May I continue?

TOMOS    Please.

LANA     She has not been ignited. Why then is she allowing
         the prayer to be chanted and the chalice to be
         raised above the great bible of sexual congress

— 21 —

when she is standing alone outside the church? No, not good, I'll have another go at that: she allows the prayer to be chanted and the chalice to be raised above the great bible of sexual congress while she stands alone outside the church. No, no, I don't like it, I still don't like it. What is she actually doing as she hears the prayer being chanted and imagines the chalice being raised above the great book – yes book, not bible – of sexual congress? She stands alone, outside the church. Again, no! Help me!

TOMOS   What are you trying to say?

LANA   I'm not sure – I – I am trying to find an effective – yet – evocative way in which to express the fact that – that – that she undervalues the importance of her own satisfaction. In addition to this, she is made aware – and not for the first time – that the emotional and physical distance between initial arousal and achievement of orgasm is much more swiftly covered in a man than in a woman yet she blames herself for this – this – discrepancy, yes I suppose you could call it that. That's it, I think – she stifles her own feelings for the sake of the male's.

TOMOS   Well, I think you just said it.

LANA   But it's so – so clinical....and I was trying to be – lyrical. Okay, long story short. She is not sexually aroused by him so why is she – pretending to be?

TOMOS   Been there, done that.

LANA   You?

— 22 —

TOMOS   A man can tell, you know.

LANA   Not in my experience.

TOMOS   It's just a question of whether he cares or not.

LANA   [A moment of thoughtful acceptance] Hmm. Where was I? Not aroused, so...

TOMOS   So why is she preten–

LANA   –Ah yes, why is she pretending to be? Answer: She has been conditioned to allow it. She has been conditioned to accept that her needs are not as important as his.

TOMOS   Conditioned?

LANA   Absolutely. Stevie Smith said it best, don't you think?

TOMOS   It would help if I knew who Steve Smith is and what he actually said.

LANA   Not Steve. Stevie. She's a woman, an English poet.

TOMOS   Oh. Well, what did she say?

LANA   If I say I am valuable and other people do not say it of me, I shall be alone...

TOMOS   I don't understand.

LANA   Try.

TOMOS   ...

LANA   The female must give in and the male must get what he wants....or she runs the risk of his losing

— 23 —

interest in her. She accepts that this is the price she must pay for being female. The desires and needs of the male are superior to the desires and needs of the female – that's the conditioning.

TOMOS   So that's what she thinks?

LANA   She does not think that, no, in fact she cat-uh-gori-cally *thinks* the opposite. But her conditioning has successfully inculcated in her the necessity to behave as if she believes it is so.

TOMOS   Ahh.

LANA   And where is her mind in all this?

TOMOS   I thought she was outside a church or something.

LANA   That was just at the beginning. Once things are – underway, shall we say – where then?

TOMOS   The Bahamas.

LANA   ...

TOMOS   Just kidding.

LANA   On the ceiling.

TOMOS   You what?

LANA   Her mind is outside her body, hovering over them, watching.

TOMOS   Now how is the audience supposed to know that?

LANA   The audience doesn't care. They are voyeurs to a man–

— 24 —

TOMOS   And to a woman.

LANA    Oh please, all play on words is strictly forbidden.

TOMOS   Well, excuse me. But you want them to know, don't you?

LANA    Yes, you're right. They must know. They would be content merely to observe and be titillated, and their blushes – if there were any – would be obscured by the darkness of the auditorium. But we must not allow them simply to – enjoy. We must let them know. In fact we must spell it out. Theatrically it is very simple. We fly a double–

TOMOS   What does that mean?

LANA    –who hovers like a ghost high above the action on the stage. One or two individuals may be sufficiently compassionate, attentive and perceptive to ask – no, it's too soon. That must come later.

TOMOS   What are you getting at?

LANA    She gazes down at herself and her suitor–

TOMOS   Suitor! That's a bit quaint.

LANA    Positively medieval. Well, what do you suggest?

TOMOS   Lover?

LANA    But love is the last thing on her mind!

TOMOS   I *am* trying to help, you know.

LANA    Of course you are. Almost done. She hovers, in her

— 25 —

mind, high above the shuddering bed with tears in her eyes. On stage, an actor of a similar shape and build, dressed as our heroine – heroine! – looks down at the writhing couple on the bed.

TOMOS    But what is she crying about?

LANA    I have no idea.

TOMOS    I don't believe that.

LANA    Shall he take her from behind?

TOMOS    Hey, that's a bit of a leap.

LANA    No. The audience must wait until act four for that. After all the descent into the black hole has only just begun. The audience must first be made to squirm and fidget before witnessing that exquisitely stimulating spectacle.

TOMOS    What a spoilsport!

LANA    The audience too must travel far enough into the black hole that all light from the entrance is lost from sight. They must make that commitment. They must be made to make that commitment. They must be made to want to make that commitment.

TOMOS    What you gonna do – chain 'em to their seats?

LANA    End of scene two.

TOMOS    Good. I'm hungry.

*END OF ACT ONE, SCENE TWO*

LANA     I left something out.

TOMOS    Well, it's too late now.

LANA     How can it be too late? I have hundreds of blank
         pages ahead of me.

TOMOS    Let's go and eat. You can put it in when we come
         back.

LANA     Is this your first....experience of being an
         assistant?

TOMOS    Yes.

LANA     You've come to it rather late in life, have you not?

TOMOS    Yes.

LANA     Would it kill you to explain?

TOMOS    Yes, it would, just at this moment.

LANA     Hmmm – touché.

                         * * *

LANA     That was good.

TOMOS    Which salsa did you like best?

LANA     The mango.

TOMOS    Me too. What was it you left out?

LANA     Mm?

TOMOS    You said you left something out of the last scene.

LANA     I presented the meat but forgot the necessary

                       — 27 —

condiments, which add so much to the enjoyment.

TOMOS   Condiments?

LANA    Easily remedied.

TOMOS   You know what your motto should be?

LANA    Hollywood has a word for them but I've forgotten
what it is.

TOMOS   *Never speak plainly when you can use a totally
obscuring metaphor*, that's what your motto should
be. Do you mean compliments?

LANA    Certainly not.

TOMOS   Insults then?

LANA    It is difficult to take you seriously sometimes. I am
trying to stimulate the audience's appetite. You
know, a little mango salsa?

TOMOS   I think you've already done that.

LANA    I'm not referring to the amuse-gueule.

TOMOS   There you go again. What's that when it's at
home?

LANA    It's a sort of – tiny little hors d'oeuvre....before
the hors d'oeuvre. Just pay attention and all will
become clear. We are coming soon enough to the
main course. A little salt then: *You have a lovely
body.*

TOMOS   I'm not sure I'm getting this. How is that salt?

— 28 —

LANA     There are no pictures in this book – I have to get them going somehow.

TOMOS   I'm completely lost now.

LANA     I'll make it scene three. No-one will know I meant to put it in earlier.

TOMOS   Whatever you say.

LANA     No, really, it's still relevant. Scene three then.

TOMOS   When you're like this you don't really care what I think, do you?

LANA     No.

## ACT ONE, SCENE THREE

LANA    They are at it again. There are a few strategically
        placed intakes of breath. Her mouth is open but
        she is unable to speak – she is too busy politely
        playing her assigned role – and her thoughts
        appear in the form of an enormous banner
        emerging from the wings. There are words on the
        banner: *I am living...*

TOMOS   Why are you whispering like that?

LANA    Those are the words on the banner: *I am living...*

TOMOS   But the audience won't be able to hear you.

LANA    Well – then let's have a soprano screech it out,
        stage left.

TOMOS   From one extreme to the other.

LANA    Just let me do it, will you. It's a stage whisper,
        okay?

TOMOS   Go ahead.

LANA    *I am living....*this statement is irrefutable – they
        are looking at her living body, after all – therefore
        utterly irrelevant. So the audience ignores it
        and continues to concentrate completely on the
        copulating couple.

TOMOS   Nice alliteration.

LANA    Thank you. Another word appears: *I am living....
        with...* Still irrelevant, if somewhat intriguing.
        There is a concluding phrase on the banner but

— 30 —

for now it remains in the wings, unseen. There are a few more gasps, a groan, a small hiatus – that quivering instant just before the male ejaculates – and then the remainder of the banner with its thus far uninteresting message emerges: *I am living....* *with* – Ah, here it is: *I am living with someone else.* The pepper!

TOMOS The what?

LANA She is living with someone else. She is already in a relationship.

TOMOS So?

LANA It's a – a – oh what is the damned word? – oh never mind. Now we have their attention again. There are shouts for mustard, vinegar, mayonnaise, brown sauce, ketchup, but it is too late. The brevity of the encounter has happily disguised the failing of the match; their lubricious juices – correction – his lubricious juices – have plugged the cracks and flaws that will later develop into chasms. This thin sauce of his disguises the dubious nature of the beef while making it appetizing and seemingly palatable....but it is on his sandwich alone, she is not hungry, hardly ever is, in fact, in situations such as this. He tastes her in the form of a sigh...

TOMOS Ah, there's the sigh.

LANA I'm glad to see you are paying attention.

TOMOS I was waiting to get back into the game if you must know. I didn't understand any of that other stuff –

— 31 —

about the dubious juices.

LANA    Sometimes one must keep going merely on faith.

TOMOS   [Mocking] Oh please, any form of preaching is strictly forbidden.

LANA    Where was I? Oh, yes. AHHH, THE HEIGHTENED APPEAL OF THE SWEET RIPE PEACH OUT OF WHICH ONE HAS BEEN ALLOWED ONLY ONE SMALL BITE.

TOMOS   Why are you yelling in that weird voice?

LANA    I'm – declaiming.

TOMOS   Sounds silly.

LANA    May I continue?

TOMOS   It's your gig.

LANA    He has had her, but only once. How many arias is that?

TOMOS   Arias?

LANA    No matter. Now we hear the sound of wheels.

TOMOS   What exactly is the sound of wheels?

LANA    I'll come to that in a minute. They are round and they roll.

TOMOS   Fascinating.

LANA    No-one is forcing you to listen to this.

TOMOS   Now wait a minute. I know I volunteered for this,

— 32 —

|       | but you need me. I know you do. |
|-------|--------------------------------|

LANA    If you say so. Sound effects are useful but are they needed here? Can't I just say 'the sound of wheels'?

TOMOS   But wheels in and of themselves do not actually make any sound. You obviously mean wheels as a – a symbol?

LANA    Do I?

TOMOS   Definitely. You're referring to travel, yes?

LANA    Perhaps I do need you...

TOMOS   You see?

LANA    Well, all right. I accept your – input. So now tell me, which approach is preferable, minimalist or megalomaniacal?

TOMOS   Wow! What syllables!

LANA    And I must not forget the black hole.

TOMOS   Your motif.

LANA    Too concrete, too concrete! End of scene. Syllables, black hole, wheels. This is all much too concrete. I must get back inside my head! End of scene, end of scene!

TOMOS   What's the matter?

LANA    I must get back inside my head, where's the entrance?

— 33 —

TOMOS   Don't get so agitated.

LANA   It's around here somewhere!

TOMOS   But you haven't described the sound of wheels.

LANA   Where is it, where is it?

TOMOS   Calm down!

LANA   Help! Help!!!!!

TOMOS   *For god's sake!*

LANA   Ah, at last! Thank christ, here it is. All is well, all is well, I'm back inside again.

TOMOS   You okay now?

LANA   My god, that was terrifying.

TOMOS   What was all that about?

LANA   Forgive me. Not now. I'll explain later. Where was I?

TOMOS   Are you sure you're all right?

LANA   Yes, yes, where was I?

TOMOS   Wheels.

LANA   Yes-yes. Wheels, the sound of which will be described later. For now, wheels carry our leading lady away – away from the black hole. How can this be?

TOMOS   Is that a rhetorical question?

— 34 —

LANA    Out of politeness – and because she is the romantic
        type – she writes words on a rectangular piece of
        card and addresses it to a destination which – how
        could she possibly foresee it! – will be hers at the
        end of....at the end of... Act five?....can that be
        right? Oh, I don't know, it might not be hers until
        the end of act forty-two for all I know!

TOMOS   Calm down. Don't get so worked up about
        everything.

LANA    I am calm. End of act one, scene three.

TOMOS   Excellent. Brava!

*END OF ACT ONE, SCENE THREE*

TOMOS   I just had a thought.

LANA    Yes?

TOMOS   The international audience.

LANA    The....international....audience...?

TOMOS   Subtitles, surtitles, whatever they're called.
        You know – translation into other languages –
        leebthingies.

LANA    Of course! Oh, I can see you are going to be
        indispensable.

TOMOS   Thank you. About time.

LANA    Um, um, um. Better make this scene four.

## ACT ONE, SCENE FOUR

LANA      Okay, you asked for this. Bearing in mind the insatiable demands of the black hole and the pervasive requirements of the international audience as a result of increasingly widespread global travel–

TOMOS      You sound like a textbook.

LANA      As I was saying: the carefully chosen words she writes–

TOMOS      That wasn't what you were saying.

LANA      Aargh! These interruptions are becoming intolerable. If only you had some idea of how an artist works, you might be a little more – a little more...

TOMOS      Understanding?

LANA      Precisely. May I continue?

TOMOS      Fire away.

LANA      The carefully chosen words she writes on the rectangular piece of ca–

TOMOS      –Are you by any chance referring to a postcard?

LANA      Yes, she is writing him a postcard.

TOMOS      Any reason why you can't just say so?

LANA      Am I to be allowed no artistic licence?

TOMOS      Describe it.

LANA    Artistic licence?

TOMOS   The postcard.

LANA    I am not sure I could stand to.

TOMOS   Remember – the power of authenticity.

LANA    I've changed my mind.

TOMOS   Just do it.

LANA    Grrrrrr. She is writing him a postcard. On
        the front of the card is an illustration of an
        indeterminate beast – no, correction, an amusing
        if slightly confusing conglomeration of certain
        recognisable parts of various beasts: the tail
        of an alligator, the body of a bear, the legs of a
        rhinoceros, the head of a horse, with a caption
        below, in a suitably bizarre font – of course –
        *Comic Sans*, so corny: *Sometimes I wonder who I am...*
        On the reverse is the continuation of this thought
        – Oh no, this is too too tedious.

TOMOS   You can't stop now!

LANA    This is the last time I shall sink this low.

TOMOS   Finish it!

LANA    On the reverse is the continuation of this thought:
        *...more often, though, I wonder what I am.* There. Is
        that whimsical enough for you?

TOMOS   It's fine! It's okay. It's kinda funny.

LANA    Kinda you to say so. Personally, I *hate* it.
        However....her carefully chosen words are

— 38 —

translated into six languages–

TOMOS   At last.

LANA   –and shown on a huge screen above the stage in addition to appearing as lines of miniscule print, wriggling across the small screens embedded in the backs of the theatre seats. Screens for patrons seated in the front row of the stalls are embedded in the vertical surface of the barrier enclosing the orchestra. The orchestra! The orchestra!

*END OF ACT ONE, SCENE FOUR*

TOMOS   What are you getting so excited about?

LANA    How could I have overlooked the orchestra!

TOMOS   Easy, you're so scattered.

LANA    I'll ignore that. The orchestra! Sixty pairs of hired hands whose owners constantly complain about their vocational anonymity and tell themselves they yearn for the glare of the concert stage but who are all secretly filled with gratitude each time they check their bank balances and blood pressure. Sixty pairs of hands, governed and guided by one pair of hands. Such odds! Such control! Such discipline! Such resentment!

TOMOS   More cynicism.

LANA    My supply is endless. Aren't you pleased? I'm just beginning to enjoy myself. How the hell do I know how a guy who scrapes horsehair across catgut for a living feels about his work? Next scene, quick. What is it – five? Six?

TOMOS   Five.

LANA    Are you sure?

TOMOS   That's what I'm here for, remember?

## ACT ONE, SCENE FIVE

LANA    A short period of darkness ensues during which we
        hear – of course! – sound effects alone – and the
        imagination, in the darkness, gets a little exercise.

TOMOS   Thoughtful of you.

LANA    A kind of intriguing gloom then, during which
        we hear wheels roll and hurtle, without pause,
        into the black hole, which must not be forgotten.
        Wheels, wheels, wheels. Constant movement.
        Destination unknown.

TOMOS   Elaborate a little – on the sounds. Since we are in
        darkness.

LANA    Wheels – movement – humankind on the move –
        mmm? Oh, yes, of course. The sound of wheels:
        they rumble–

TOMOS   –Double basses.

LANA    What?

TOMOS   A job for the double basses – rumbling.

LANA    Oh. Yes. Good. Rumble. Double basses. Yes. Where
        was I? They rumble because the road is rough, the
        load is heavy and progress is slow; they thunder
        – heavy vehicles moving at high speeds; they hiss
        because the streets are wet with rain; they squeal....
        sharp bends, and so on. Let the instruments fight
        that out amongst themselves. End of scene five.

*END OF ACT ONE, SCENE FIVE*

— 41 —

TOMOS   Good.

LANA   No quibbles about brevity?

TOMOS   No.

LANA   I'm exhausted.

TOMOS   It's odd, but that scene made me sad.

LANA   Yes....?

TOMOS   Were you being a bit maudlin?

LANA   Possibly....so....what should come next, d'you think?

TOMOS   I think it's time we knew a little more about our central characters, our – agonists – what they look like, how they feel – you know.

LANA   You're probably right.

TOMOS   No *probably* about it.

LANA   All righty. I'll go along with what you say.

TOMOS   Good.

LANA   Two 'good's. I must be improving.

TOMOS   No, I'm becoming more accepting.

LANA   Oh, is that it. Pleasure is always so short-lived.

TOMOS   You may be exhausted but you sound as if you're in high spirits.

LANA   One must...

— 42 —

TOMOS  Yes?

LANA  One must strike – before the iron – freezes.

TOMOS  Weird thing to say.

LANA  It's a quote.

TOMOS  What kind of weirdo would say a thing like that? Why are you smiling?

LANA  Doesn't matter. Let's move on.

TOMOS  Okay. Scene six.

LANA  A weirdo called – oh, never mind.

TOMOS  Weird.

# ACT ONE, SCENE SIX

LANA  Let one of the two be sad. Let it be he. He is forever trying – unsuccessfully – to grasp the butterfly of happiness which continually flutters out of reach.

TOMOS  Hey, why not show that – the butterflies an' all.

LANA  No....one butterfly, only one.

TOMOS  But just think – a whole – you know – oh, what's the word – for a bunch of butterflies...

LANA  I don't know – a swarm? – a flurry? – a gaggle? – a flutter? – a flap?

TOMOS  Whatever. Can't you see it? Dozens of beautiful butterflies fluttering about?

LANA  Yes, I can see it. But I don't want it.

TOMOS  But it works!

LANA  May I continue?

TOMOS  ...

LANA  He stands in the middle of the stage, alone, the stage is bare. Suddenly a butterfly appears. One of the most beautiful species, blue, gold, black, it is exquisite. He–

TOMOS  The people at the back won't see it.

LANA  He moves towards it–

TOMOS  They won't!

— 44 —

LANA       Each time he moves towards it, it flutters out of
           reach. He sighs, he – oh hell, you're right. It will
           be nothing but a speck, a mote.

TOMOS   Why not project an image of the butterfly onto the
           back wall of the stage? Blown up really big so we
           can see the shape, the wings, the colours.

LANA       That's rather lovely, yes. Obvious, but lovely.

TOMOS   And I still think you should have a – a – gaggle or
           giggle or whatever it is.

LANA       All right! We'll have all that!

TOMOS   Don't yell at me!

LANA       Sorry!

TOMOS   I'll just go, shall I?

LANA       No, please don't go. I'm sorry, but....I'm tired and
           it's just that....I didn't want to dwell on this....and
           now it's taking so long.

TOMOS   Well I think you're just about there. What else did
           you want to say?

LANA       Every time he tries to grasp one of the butterflies,
           it flutters out of reach but he *keeps trying* until
           finally, he stops and slumps onto the stage, head in
           hands. Let us leave him there....while we describe
           the quality of his sadness. We do this by–

TOMOS   Why don't you take a break?

LANA       A break?

— 45 —

TOMOS   You said you were tired.

LANA    I am....but I have so much to do. So much to say.

TOMOS   If you take a break you'll come back refreshed. Just leave him there.

LANA    ...Was that enough to constitute a scene? The butterflies, the slumping?

TOMOS   It constituted a fine scene.

LANA    All right. But you have to help me get back into this when I return.

TOMOS   I told you. That's what I'm here for.

*END OF ACT ONE, SCENE SIX*

TOMOS   Here, stretch out on the sofa for a while.

LANA    All right....you know, I'm not sleeping well these
        days.

TOMOS   I'm not surprised. It's the pressure. It's a lot to
        handle.

LANA    The pressure....yes....ahhh, that feels wonderful.
        Don't let me sleep too long, will you.

TOMOS   I won't.

LANA    The butterfly idea was really good. I think it will
        work.

TOMOS   Yes, I think so too....[*watches as she begins to drift
        off*]....you know, I daren't show it....but I really
        like you.

LANA    Mm?

TOMOS   Nothing.

                            * * *

TOMOS   Feeling a bit better?

LANA    Much. Where was I?

TOMOS   One of them is sad.

LANA    Yes, yes. Next scene – which one is it now?

TOMOS   Seven.

                          — 47 —

# ACT ONE, SCENE SEVEN

LANA    Start with joy – no, no, this is a man devoid of joy. Pleasure then, carnal pleasure especially – yes, that should cover it – thrown into relief by its absence the way white is thrown into relief by adjacent black. The stage is black, yes, with one bright light piercing the gloom.

TOMOS   Are you sure?

LANA    I am trying to explain a simple idea: there is no white more blinding, startling or unequivocal than the white surrounded by an expanse of black–

TOMOS   –But how will they get the connection? How will the audience know what you're symbolising? They will just see this bright light–

LANA    –Similarly, there is no pleasure more....more.... uplifting – no; piercing – nope; intense – no – oh hell, what is the word? – no pleasure more – dumty-dumty-dum – no pleasure more – what is the word! – we shall find it in a moment – no – what is the right word! What IS it?

TOMOS   Don't get so worked up.

LANA    You have no idea how difficult this is!

TOMOS   Well, I'm sorry but....just try and keep moving forward, as best you can.

LANA    [*Deep breath*] All right. All right. Similarly....you'll like this, I promise. Similarly, there is no joy more–

— 48 —

TOMOS   –Pleasure.

LANA    What?

TOMOS   Pleasure. You were going to use the word pleasure, not joy.

LANA    Oh yes. Grazie. No pleasure more – and I'll find the right word in a minute–

TOMOS   Unbearable?

LANA    That's it!!! Perfect! So you are on my side?

TOMOS   Completely.

LANA    Marvellous. Okay – unbearable – where was I?

TOMOS   No pleasure more unbearable.

LANA    That isn't the right word...

TOMOS   Then just leave a sp–

LANA    –But!....it will do for now. No joy–

TOMOS   Pleasure!

LANA    Oh, yes – I'm hopeless, aren't I? – pleasure – no pleasure more – unbearable – than that experienced in the midst of an all-pervading – umm – oh hell, I'm stuck again.

TOMOS   This is impossible.

LANA    Let me start from the beginning....please...

TOMOS   Go ahead.

— 49 —

LANA     Similarly, there is no pleasure more....unbearable
         – no [*distressed*] it isn't what I mean....than that
         experienced in the midst of an all-pervading....but
         [*greater distress*] after all that, how can I depict it on
         stage....[*starts to sob*]

TOMOS   Are you all right?

LANA     [*Small voice*] I'm exhausted.

TOMOS   *You're* exhausted.

LANA     [*Smaller voice*] Tyrants....they're such tyrants.

TOMOS   Who are?

LANA     [*Smallest voice*] Words.

TOMOS   I know. I'm sorry.

LANA     I simply must get to the end of this thought or – or
         – I'm afraid I might die.

TOMOS   Don't be silly.

LANA     You're right, I'm ridiculous.

TOMOS   I didn't say that.

LANA     [*Recovering*] It's what you're thinking though, I
         know it is.

TOMOS   It's temporary.

LANA     I am temporarily ridiculous – that rolls off the
         tongue, does it not? I like that. Temporarily
         ridiculous.

TOMOS   My god, you're – you're – like a–

— 50 —

LANA    I'm like the weather, constantly changing – yes, you're absolutely right. All right, crisis over. I am calm now. There is no white more....blinding.... than that surrounded by an expanse of black. Similarly, there is no pleasure more – seductive – no, but press on regardless – no pleasure more – insert correct but presently unavailable word – no blah-blah-blah – than that experienced in the midst of....of...

TOMOS  Yes?

LANA    I have it. At last.

TOMOS  Thank god.

LANA    Consoling.

TOMOS  That's it?

LANA    Oh blessed relief, yes. No pleasure more consoling than that experienced in the midst of anguish.

TOMOS  Are you sure that's it?

LANA    Yes. Thus the man. He has been consoled by her ability to provide relief from his anguish. For him, the woman is his light, his salvation, his inspiration – the provider of everything that he lacks and is unable to provide for himself. She is a cornucopia of consolation. Only she can make him feel whole. And I have no idea how to show all that on stage...

TOMOS  More butterflies?

LANA    Hardly.

— 51 —

TOMOS   Okay, okay. And for her?

LANA    Mm?

TOMOS   What is he for her?

LANA    Oh, you know, the usual. Just another infatuated mick who's about to get another charity fuck.

TOMOS   How sweet. Isn't it possible that he represents everything that she is not?

LANA    Absolutely not.

TOMOS   It is a tragedy then.

LANA    I believe we have already established that. He is the fire that will *burn her up*. But, as with fucking from the rear, we have to wait until act whatever-it-is to find that out. As for the soundtrack, the modernity of the music demands that she is a bell, one clear note without a rhythm while he is an idiophone.

TOMOS   A what!

LANA    An instrument of percussion. A block of smooth hard wood, teak perhaps, expertly rapped in an urgent highly complicated rhythm without tune – no, change that: an urgent highly complicated tuneless rhythm. Yes, that's it. This is the section of the score for the successful execution of which the percussionist has spent an abstemious twenty-four hours.

TOMOS   I like that word.

LANA    What was I saying....what did you say?

— 52 —

TOMOS   Percussion. It's one of those – what-you-ma-call-its
        – isn't it? – when the word sounds like what it is.

LANA    Onomatopoeia?

TOMOS   What a bloody awful word!

LANA    But that's what I was saying earlier! They're
        tyrants!

TOMOS   You said soundtrack.

LANA    What?

TOMOS   A minute ago, you called the music the soundtrack.
        So is it a movie?

LANA    Just a minor slip of the tongue. Back to the story,
        do you mind? Let us review briefly their earlier
        contact. Their conversation–

TOMOS   Post-coital?

LANA    Post– ? Oh. If you like.

TOMOS   Well, you had them copulate so is the conversation
        before or after that?

LANA    Both. It's not important. You decide. Their
        conversation is half truth, half lies – or, more
        accurately, three quarters truth, one quarter
        lies. She is the one incapable of being completely
        candid.

TOMOS   Sounds pre- to me.

LANA    Will you please stop interrupting!

— 53 —

TOMOS  I'll just raise my hand when I want to say
something, shall I?

LANA  ...

TOMOS  Wow, I think that's what they call a withering
look.

LANA  Think of it as an impassioned appeal for silence.
Where was I? Her inability to be completely
truthful – this is easily fathomed because, as is
clear to a perceptive onlooker, she could crush him
with the truth. Perhaps her subconscious knows
this. Perhaps it is her habit. Be all that as it may,
once he has pawed her body (more gently than is
his true inclination – he is not immune to the need
to impress), the irritant has been deposited within
his brain: he has had her, now it is imperative she
become available for having on a permanent basis.
She fills up the inexplicable void in his being. She,
on the other hand, swallows down her initial shock
at the sight of his spindleshanks since he has the
necessary protuberance that proves that he, if not
exactly manly, is in fact a man. But the story must
progress with – what's that word I was looking for
earlier?

TOMOS  [*Weary*] Not again.

LANA  Complications! That's the word I was looking for.
At last. The story must now have complications,
therefore they must part. End of scene seven.

TOMOS  And I need a drink.

*END OF ACT ONE, SCENE SEVEN*

— 54 —

LANA     Are you unhappy?

TOMOS  Sort of.

LANA     Would you like to take a break?

TOMOS  I'd like a coffee and perhaps a brandy.

LANA     Go and have one then.

TOMOS  Do you want anything?

LANA     No, you go on your own. Take your time, come back when you're ready.

TOMOS  You're sure you can manage without me for a while?

LANA     I'm certain.

TOMOS  Okay. Back in a bit. [*Exits*]

LANA     ...Alone at last....ah, the joy of solitude...

* * *

TOMOS  I'm b-a-c-k! There's a really good coffee bar just round the corner from here.

LANA     Is there. Good. Act one, scene eight. Other male protuberances have–

TOMOS  Wait! Hold on a minute, let me take my coat off!

LANA     Well, hurry up.

TOMOS  Okay, I'm ready.

# ACT ONE, SCENE EIGHT

LANA    Act one, scene eight. Other male protuberances have nosed their way into her cavity. Ah, the treasures there....the flushed pink skin, the slime, the stagnant rock-pool smell–

TOMOS    I'm not sure I'm going to enjoy this.

LANA    The smooth surfaces, firm yet yielding....the capacity for accommodation! ...*And*, whispers a female audience member to her companion in the adjacent seat, *the price of accommodation?* The fact is, the whisperer has recently written a metaphysical poem on this very subject with this very phrase as its title.

TOMOS    Very subject? Very phrase? I don't get it. How does that fit in?

LANA    The woman who has just whispered this to her friend has recently written a poem in which she expressed the high personal cost to herself of allowing the men in her life to call the shots, dictate the rules and generally ride roughshod over her feelings and aspirations.

TOMOS    What was that phrase again?

LANA    The price of accommodation.

TOMOS    And that's the title of the poem?

LANA    Yes.

TOMOS    I like that.

LANA    So do I. So let's take a look at them, the men who–

TOMOS   Because it's got two meanings, hasn't it?

LANA    Yes it has. The literal and the metaphorical.

TOMOS   There you go again, making simple things complicated.

LANA    I am simply labelling things correctly.

TOMOS   Tosh. You're just showing off.

LANA    ...

TOMOS   It's no good getting huffy. You know I'm right.

LANA    May I please continue? Where was I?

TOMOS   The men who.

LANA    Ah yes. Let us take a look at the other men who have....uhhh....insinuated themselves into her. A motley collection, they process across the stage: one is simply an overgrown baby, wearing only a nappy and sucking his thumb, he looks very innocent, self-conscious and foolish; after him comes a true bohemian, long hair, faded clothing, no shoes, unwashed; then comes a studious type with spectacles and serious expression, he has bad posture and carries an armful of books; after them we have a couple of men who look as if they work on a building site, they have tools hanging off their belts and hammers in their hands, they look like friends, they are chatting and grinning and every few minutes one of them gives a loud wolf whistle and they both make lewd gestures; they are

— 57 —

followed by a sporty type in exercise gear; and one in a monk's habit–

TOMOS  Never!

LANA  Why not? No-one is immune to the urges of the sexual appetite, the clergy least of all – have you read the newspapers lately! The monk is followed by a couple of nondescripts, a short one with a compact body and the shifty expression of a salesman; lastly, a rather elegant one in evening dress, suave and superior, who stands out from the rest, as well he might, being tall, black and extremely handsome. A baker's dozen, all under thirty, all capable of fathering a child, they parade across the stage, an entertaining cross-section of manhood, like contestants in a Miss Universe contest.

TOMOS  Miss Universe? They're men!

LANA  Sorry. I couldn't resist.

TOMOS  So she's had all those guys?

LANA  No, they have had her, important distinction. And they are merely symbols. No, not symbols...

TOMOS  Types. Stereotypes.

LANA  Yes. In fact, as I'm in the mood to hammer the point home, after the parade of these humans, let's have another parade, one in which black-garbed stage-hands carry life-sized cardboard cut-outs across the brightly-lit stage to demonstrate the two-dimensionality of these has-beens – and that

— 58 —

|        | should be enough hyphens for even the keenest fan. |
|--------|---|
| TOMOS | I just had a really wicked idea. |
| LANA | Yes? |
| TOMOS | Why not give the cardboard cut-outs really – you know – like – really big protruberances. |
| LANA | Protuberances. |
| TOMOS | Whatever. |
| LANA | Oh, that is wicked, I like it. No – it's too crude. |
| TOMOS | Yeah, I guess it is. |
| LANA | For once you agree with me. |
| TOMOS | Okay, I have another idea. Not crude. |
| LANA | Y-e-s? |
| TOMOS | Why not call it The High Price of Accommodation? |
| LANA | What? |
| TOMOS | It's a better title, don't you think? – for the poem – The High Price of Accommodation? |
| LANA | It's too literal. Too....obvious. |
| TOMOS | Is it a real poem? An actual poem? |
| LANA | Perhaps. |
| TOMOS | What do you mean, *perhaps*? If I am to be of any use at all you have to be completely open and |

honest with me.

LANA    No I don't.

TOMOS    You do!

LANA    Oh all *right*. It's included in an anthology of poems which takes its title from that particular poem and that's all I'm going to say.

TOMOS    Really? By whom?

LANA    ...Me, if you must know.

TOMOS    Ah...

LANA    What do you mean, *Ah*...?

TOMOS    Published?

LANA    No. Can we please get on now?

TOMOS    May I read them?

LANA    No.

TOMOS    Why not?

LANA    Can we please get back to the–

TOMOS    I just want to get to know you!

LANA    You're upsetting me.

TOMOS    Why? I love poetry!

LANA    Not now. Please!!

TOMOS    Okay-okay. No need to shout.

LANA     You have no idea how hard this is for me.

TOMOS   Help me understand then. Let me read your
         poetry.

LANA     I beg you–

TOMOS   I am trying to understand. I want to understand.

LANA     Could we – please, just – get back to the story.

TOMOS   Okay, go ahead. There's no need to cry.

LANA     I – I – appreciate your enthusiasm, I really do, but
         I can't stand th–

TOMOS   –The interruptions.

LANA     The *memories.*

TOMOS   Sorry. Get back to the procession then. Go on, I'll
         behave, I promise.

LANA     ...I think I had come to the end of it.

TOMOS   What next then?

LANA     They part.

TOMOS   The man and the woman?

LANA     Yes. They have parted.

TOMOS   No post-coital ciggy?

LANA     It doesn't fit here. And anyway, they don't smoke.
         End of scene – whatever it is.

TOMOS   Eight. Good. Very good, well done.

— 61 —

LANA     Thank you.

TOMOS   I thought you could use a little encouragement.

*END OF ACT ONE, SCENE EIGHT*

TOMOS  You okay now?

LANA   Yes, I'm fine.

TOMOS  Perhaps you ought to take a break.

LANA   You think?

TOMOS  You got pretty upset back there. You don't want to
       push yourself too hard.

LANA   No, I have to do this. It won't stop being torture
       just because I take a break. So where are we?

TOMOS  But there is so much for the audience to take in.
       Give *them* a break, at least.

LANA   No, there's one more scene in this act, then that's
       it.

TOMOS  Very well.

LANA   All right, where are we?

TOMOS  Scene nine.

LANA   Are you ready for more details?

TOMOS  Details? Absolutely.

# ACT ONE, SCENE NINE

LANA   On opposite sides of the stage we see two objects, mail receptacles, one stage right, a painted metal box about the size of a large shoebox, with a curved top and a front flap the shape of a miniature portcullis. Slotted into the side of the box is a narrow flat strip of metal that can be elevated to serve as a crude flag and the box is fixed on a metal pole about three feet high. A square-shaped, slow-moving vehicle stops beside it, an arm reaches out, lowers the portcullis flap, removes a thick white envelope from within and tosses a small blue envelope inside.

TOMOS   [Sings] Wait, oh yeah, wait a minute, Mr. Postman!

LANA   Exactly. Such lack of sophistication.

TOMOS   Who, me?

LANA   No the makers of this contraption. The other one–

TOMOS   The other what?

LANA   The other mail receptacle.

TOMOS   Oh – right.

LANA   The other, stage left, is a rectangular opening cut into the middle of a heavy wooden high-gloss-painted door which has a panel of Victorian era stained glass decorating its upper half. A figure in a postal delivery uniform appears, carrying a large canvas bag, bandolero-style across his body. He removes a white envelope from the bag and pushes

— 64 —

it through the letterbox of this London house.

TOMOS  What London house?

LANA  That's where she lives, our liebhaberin.

TOMOS  She does? You might have told us that before, you know.

LANA  I might have, but I didn't. We hear the light slapping sound as the letter lands inside, flat on the bare wooden floorboards of the house hallway. It's a long letter, extra postage was needed. We return to the other mailbox. The slow square vehicle rolls up again, an arm reaches out again, pulls down the portcullis-shaped front flap of the American mailbox, removes the outgoing letter lying there and tosses a letter inside – we hear the faint metallic resonance as the edge of the envelope hits the back of the box – if the audience is quiet enough. Then the portcullis is closed and the vehicle moves off.

TOMOS  Oh, I get it. They are writing letters – pretty quaint. This is before e-mail, right?

LANA  Long before. Haven't you looked at the programme?

TOMOS  I never look at the programme.

LANA  You never look at the–

TOMOS  –Cut it out. I'm a pleb, okay? Don't rub it in.

LANA  Very well. I continue. These mundane events are replicated and the resulting sounds are repeated

— 65 —

via sound recording until the frequency of the repetitions creates a muffled but insistent rhythm, regularly irregular – or is it irregularly regular? – that becomes more and more urgent, until it is a jarring drumbeat.

TOMOS   Cool!

LANA   Ironic – no, that's not the word–

TOMOS   –Not again!

LANA   It's an occupational hazard. Haven't you accepted that yet?

TOMOS   Yeah, yeah.

LANA   May I continue? Ironic – it will do for now – that the raw material for this section of the script was created entirely by words yet this interlude is wordless; what arises is a kind of jungly song without words which–

TOMOS   –So they've parted and they are writing each other letters – lots of letters.

LANA   Yes, lots of letters. Paradoxical! That's it. But wait – again there is a disturbance in the wings – a swell of voices high and low, culminating in a kind of vocal swoon which begins to fade until all sound ceases. A few moments of silence then we begin to hear, issuing from the wings, stage left, a low moaning and some short whispered mutterings – the female – and, stage right, rapid panting and guttural outbursts – the male – that accompany mastur – no – let's call it....self-love.

— 66 —

TOMOS   I'll say this, you're fearless. Cynical but fearless.

LANA    Thanks.

TOMOS   And a bit of a moaner.

LANA    I'll forget you said that. Where was I? We can only
        imagine the turgid penis stage right, the swollen
        labia stage left, the frotting hands and the–

TOMOS   Frotting?

LANA    Yes.

TOMOS   Is that a word?

LANA    It is now. Oh hell, I've lost my place again! I'll
        have to start all over!

TOMOS   How convenient.

LANA    What do you mean? Oh, never mind, I know very
        well what you mean.

TOMOS   I was joking!

LANA    Your low opinion of me is really very galling.
        Penis, labia, frotting – ah yes, here it is, the final
        spasm that opens the internal floodgates of arousal,
        makes the heart pound, the legs rigid and releases
        all tension that has accumulated. We throw both
        bodies, flailing, their blood slowly redistributing
        itself throughout their sated bodies, into the black
        hole. Whew! End of act one, I think.

TOMOS   Definitely.

                *END OF ACT ONE, SCENE NINE*

                        — 67 —

TOMOS   Suggestion!

LANA    Yes?

TOMOS   You probably won't like this but I'm going to say it
        anyway.

LANA    Yes?

TOMOS   Projections.

LANA    Oh not again.

TOMOS   Just a thought!

LANA    ....No – wait – in fact you've inspired me – not
        projections but...

TOMOS   Yes?

LANA    Actual people – actors.

TOMOS   Yes?

LANA    Engaged in committing these salacious acts stage
        left and stage right.

TOMOS   Woh, that's pushing it a bit.

LANA    Well – let's push it!

TOMOS   Well okay then!

ACT TWO

## ACT TWO, SCENE ONE

LANA    So – a few more details about our – central beings.

TOMOS  Yes please.

LANA    Okay, let us examine our protagonists a little more closely.

TOMOS  We don't even know the colour of their hair or their eyes or anything.

LANA    Him: brown-brown; her: red-grey. End of scene.

*END OF ACT TWO, SCENE ONE*

TOMOS   I *hate* it when you're cryptic.

LANA    That's because you don't like being forced to use your brain.

TOMOS   I use my brain. Anyway, it's not up to you whether I use my brain or not. You're not in charge of my brain!

LANA    God forbid.

TOMOS   You might as well write in Morse code if you're going to be that cryptic. I won't be the only reader who won't like it, I can tell you that.

LANA    There is no reader.

TOMOS   It's cruelty on your part. Why couldn't you explain it nicely?

LANA    *Nicely?*

TOMOS   You see what's happened here?

LANA    Oh yes, I see. We have completely departed from the matter in hand.

TOMOS   If you'd used a few more words in the first place, we wouldn't have subsequently wasted so many words discussing it.

LANA    I do not like wasting words. You appear to be in agreement about that.

TOMOS   Perhaps it would be a good thing now and then if you did.

LANA    Now you seem to be saying that I *should* waste

— 70 —

words?

TOMOS   Forget it. You can tie me in knots if you like, I
know what I'm saying.

LANA   I'm glad one of us is so certain. That was very nice
use of the word 'subsequently', by the way.

TOMOS   Don't try and get round me now.

LANA   Look, why don't we start all over again?

TOMOS   Good idea. So – I have a question – may I? Ask? A
question?

LANA   Feel free.

TOMOS   I thought you said her pubic hair was light brown.

LANA   And so it is.

TOMOS   But you said red-grey.

LANA   I did.

TOMOS   So – she dyes her hair – her head hair?

LANA   Correct.

TOMOS   Red.

LANA   Yes. Bright red.

TOMOS   I think the audience would like to know a bit more
about that – the women at least.

LANA   Certainly. Let's have a brief scene with our
heroine, her head slathered–

— 71 —

TOMOS   New scene!

LANA   Oops, yes.

# ACT TWO, SCENE TWO

LANA  Here is our heroine, her head slathered in what looks like mud.

TOMOS  Mud!

LANA  Henna. Red henna.

TOMOS  Is that like a shampoo?

LANA  It's a powder, ground-up something or other – you mix it with water, though it does not dissolve, then you plaster it on your damp hair. It is messy – like gritty mud – but it's natural, so it does not damage the hair.

TOMOS  No peroxide, no ammonia, no sulfates, no paraben. Not tested on animals.

LANA  Can we please move along here?

TOMOS  You sound like a bus conductor!

LANA  Any more fares, any more fares now, *please*.

TOMOS  I was beginning to think you had lost your sense of humour...

LANA  Are you kidding? You have to have a sense of humour to write this rot.

TOMOS  We should probably get back to the story.

LANA  Gladly. She walks across the stage with her head slathered in henna-mud and exits to the sounds of running water.

TOMOS   What about some close-ups at this point?

LANA   Close-ups?

TOMOS   Yeah, you know, with those big screens they use –
so the audience can see details – faces, close-ups –
yes? The people sitting at the back, I mean.

LANA   Yes, yes, good.

TOMOS   And what about some music?

LANA   Of course, we need music.

TOMOS   Yeah, the guys in the orchestra will have fallen
asleep by now.

LANA   They are probably glad of the rest. Dido's lament.
Perfect. Let us now–

TOMOS   –For a minute there I thought you were going to
say, Let us now pray!

LANA   Not a chance. Let us now, to the tune of Dido's
exquisite lament, examine their extremities.

TOMOS   I don't know that one.

LANA   Henry Purcell.... Carthage....*Remember me*....
heartbreaking....

*END OF ACT TWO, SCENE TWO*

TOMOS    Better put that in the programme.

LANA     Naturally, though why bother, when *some* people don't even read their programmes.

TOMOS    Don't start.

LANA     What? Oh, the music....oh no, I can't do this, I – I – oh....the pain is unbearable....I – can't, I can't....the music, it breaks my heart, oh...

TOMOS    What's wrong?

LANA     The pain....in the music....the beauty, the eternal strife, the – the – the – oh I simply cannot....I have to be alone....I must be alone in the dark...

TOMOS    You want me to leave?

LANA     Either that or keep silent.

TOMOS    You're trembling!

LANA     I must have silence [*breathing speeds up*] I must be alone.

TOMOS    I'll leave you alone for a while, shall I? Ten minutes?

LANA     Make it fifteen. No – don't go! Don't leave me!

TOMOS    I'll just step outside for a few minutes. I won't go anywhere, I'll be on the other side of that door, okay?

LANA     All right....thank you.

TOMOS    If you need me just tap on the door. [*Exits*]

LANA      ...Alone – [*deep breath*] oh, bliss. I'll just close
          my eyes for a few moments. Blackness and
          silence – it's like a drug to me...ahhhh, peace at
          last. [*Enormous sigh*] And....here they come....
          my thoughts, here they come, barging in like
          uninvited guests, chattering, getting drunk,
          knocking over precious ornaments, muddying the
          carpet and leaving fingerprints on the mirrors. I'll
          carry on in spite of them, dammit. Where was I?
          I must describe the male and the female. That's
          it – an examination of their extremities. So much
          information contained in the hands – and feet.
          I'll talk about their hands first. Their hands have
          already made contact, each pair of hands with
          certain areas of the other's body – mostly those
          connected with reproduction – ah, the drive to
          create another pair of tiny hands. How dull sexual
          coupling would be without the use of the hands.

TOMOS    My best friend's mother said the most exciting
          thing about a man is his hands.

LANA      What are you doing here?!

TOMOS    I was listening at the door and you only needed
          fifteen seconds, not fifteen minutes. Do you think
          that's true – about a man's hands?

LANA      No.

TOMOS    Well, you should know. What about her hands?

LANA      She has the hands of a milkmaid.

TOMOS    Meaning?

— 76 —

LANA    Average size, square palm, strong fingers, long
        lifeline.

TOMOS   Do milkmaids usually have long lifelines?

LANA    Probably.

TOMOS   Aha – artistic licence.

LANA    I'm so tired.

TOMOS   I'll be quiet. Are you ready to go on?

LANA    Yes. Where were we?

TOMOS   Act two, scene three, I believe.

LANA    Thank you.

TOMOS   I am trying, you know.

LANA    I know.

## ACT TWO, SCENE THREE

LANA    Two naked bodies in the gloom of a sparsely-furnished room with thin sheets and thin curtains, silently writhing. The room is not warm. She is giving herself to him. That's the way it is: a woman gives herself to a man, a woman is taken. She gives, he takes. Misgivings arise in her along with the conviction that this must happen. The point is, for her there were no other choices because she does not know what it means to choose. She is always the chosen and there has never been a shortage of choosers. She is in the habit of accepting the guidance of fate. Therefore she has accepted this. They were thrown together, their lives collided – *they* collided – in the shabby hallway of a mediocre rooming house in an insignificant town in one of the less populated states of a large continent....Are you all right? What's the matter?

TOMOS   I don't know – it sounds so – so jaded. I can't help it, listening to that...

LANA    Jaded? No that's not the word.

TOMOS   Whatever, it made me sad.

LANA    Callous?

TOMOS   That's worse! I'm not sure I can stand this. It's–

LANA    No-one is forcing you to stay.

TOMOS   But you need me....don't you?

LANA    I think so. Yes.

— 78 —

TOMOS   Aren't you sure?

LANA    Of course I need you....and don't forget it's only a
        story. Art is always worse than real life. I'm sorry
        but I have to get on here. Please stay.

TOMOS   Go ahead. I'll feel better in a minute.

LANA    What I am trying to describe is life itself. It is –
        natural.

TOMOS   I like that much better. But you don't mean it in a
        good way, do you? Natural – I know you – that's
        worse than anything, right?

LANA    Perhaps. I'll keep mum on that one. I'm going to
        continue now.

TOMOS   Go on then.

LANA    They are stripped bare – no – rather, they are
        willingly unclothed. The skin – their skin – will
        play a very great role in this ramble as it curls and
        scorches and flies into the black hole. We note
        that his has a purplish-pink cast denoting poor
        circulation and lack of health while hers has the
        faint glow and golden hue of good health. She may
        be small but she is sturdy. Her skin is smooth, she
        looks slightly....burnished. On the huge screens
        we see a close-up of his hands as he moves them
        over her body – burnishing her still further.

TOMOS   Nice.

LANA    But the burnishing is only in her mind. Her mind
        is aware of one thing, her body another. Her

— 79 —

innermost desire is to be caressed as if her skin were made of silken fur, which would make her swoon, but her body is being handled as if she were a lump of soft dough, there to be grasped and kneaded. The curtain suddenly drops. The audience roars its objection – NO!!!!! But we have been moving along too quickly. Tension allowed to build to such a pitch demands release but – for her – there is none. The audience must be made to feel that.

*END OF ACT TWO, SCENE THREE*

TOMOS   What's happening now? I'm a bit lost.

LANA    She was not aroused by his touch. They had sex,
        she didn't come. End of scene.

TOMOS   I don't know why I spend a single second worrying
        about you – you have a heart of stone.

LANA    I do! I do!

TOMOS   I thought you were going to describe our two –
        whatever you're calling them now – their physical
        features.

LANA    Bring in the ballet!

TOMOS   What?!

LANA    For humour – comic relief.

TOMOS   Oh yes, that should have them rolling in the aisles.
        You have a very perverse sense of timing, you
        know that?

# ACT TWO, SCENE FOUR

LANA    No pink tutus, no flesh-coloured hose, rather the dancers are clothed in tight stretchy shiny black stuff, from the base of the neck all the way down to wrists and ankles. White stitching along the lines of autopsy. A dozen dancers. Bare feet. They move skilfully around the edge of the black hole and the question is: Will they fall/topple/tumble/flop/hurl/fling themselves or be otherwise propelled – but what's left? – in?

TOMOS    I like this, this is good.

LANA    The precision and certainty of their movements – the strenuous nature of a dancer's training is notorious – belies the uncertainty of their fate. Trained to the highest standard, they are enslaved by the demands of choreography that has been stringently rehearsed to convey – what's the word? – danger? – no, it'll come to me – stringently rehearsed in order to convey blah-blah-blah. So we are unnerved and become anxious when one of the women appears to fall backwards. Will one of the men be there to catch her? Are they meant to look as if they are making up these steps and movements as they go along? Are we allowed to laugh? When one of the men falters, will another man or perhaps two women be there to support him? The whole company teeters in unison – are they about to they topple en masse and stagger to their knees? Or will the dancers recover and avert a complete collapse? Ah, the joys of precariousness – that's the word! – pre-carious-

— 82 —

ness....and oh, the power this state has over
the breath; something that inhibits the natural
involuntary function of exhaling must be worth
watching, even without contemplation. Is anyone
in this audience actually contemplating the action
on the stage – they are a collection of upholstered
sponges. The sound of the orchestra surges,
forte, fortissimo, fortississimo, Stravinskyesque,
Rite-like, adding to the tension. Again, the
percussionist is stretched to his limit: *Christ, here
we go again*, he thinks as he readies himself for
the onslaught. Surrounded by the instruments of
his trade – no, not trade, art – surrounded by the
instruments of his art, he thinks, *I could murder a
pint*, and he will, after the show. Several in fact. Or
perhaps the percussionist is a woman – one should
not be shocked by such conditioned thinking but
one is – ever so slightly....admit it. We leave them
now, the twelve dancers, jungling along, because
this dance, once started, will never end. That is
what we are meant to understand. This dance
never ends. The music fades. The dance continues
in silence. Perhaps this part of the stage revolves,
transporting the riot to another unseen part of the
stage. Go to black.

*END OF ACT TWO, SCENE FOUR*

TOMOS   That was terrific!

LANA    Colour and movement, that's what they like.

TOMOS   You seem to be getting into your stride now.
        You're rolling.

LANA    Yes. Certainty speeds things up.

TOMOS   And yet...

LANA    And yet?

TOMOS   What you were describing was uncertainty.

LANA    But with certainty.

TOMOS   Okay, what's next?

LANA    A car journey. Wheels again.

TOMOS   Good.

LANA    By the end of this production dozens, no, hundreds
        – no – *thousands* of wheels will have been hurled (or
        have rolled of their own accord) into the black hole,
        which shows absolutely no sign of becoming full.

TOMOS   But that's the nature of a black hole, isn't it?
        Never to become full.

LANA    You did not split your infinitive. You cannot know
        what that means to me.

TOMOS   As I was saying – it's more a kind of – passage to
        somewhere else, isn't it?

LANA    Yes, you're right. I was being unnecessarily lyrical.

— 84 —

TOMOS   Inaccurate is what I call it.

LANA    Same thing. Zips!

TOMOS   What now? You've perked up suddenly.

LANA    Because the words are coming. Happiness is when words flow unbidden.

TOMOS   Oh no, you're being poetic again.

LANA    Zips also have a starring role. Zips, large and small, and the sound they make when opened and closed. Let us hear that now, like a miniature overture to a new chapter, the sound of wheels and zips. The music is very modern, I already mentioned that, I think.

TOMOS   Positively avantgarde.

LANA    Yes, a brief musical introduction, the conductor waves his arms around – that always impresses everyone – everyone except the orchestra, that is – and then we find our two – what have I been calling them?!

TOMOS   All sorts of things.

LANA    That's not very helpful.

TOMOS   Why don't you give them names, for chrissake?

LANA    Names! Brilliant!!

TOMOS   Honestly, sometimes you are unbelievably backward.

LANA    Um, um, um, let me see....Olive, Enid, Sara,

— 85 —

Josephine, Alice, Mary, Caroline, Louise, Joanna, Nellie, Patricia, Diane....um, um, um... Frederick, John, Brian, Nigel, Albert, Simon, George, Marvin, Sidney. Any good?

TOMOS   Well, which are you going to use?

LANA   All of them!

TOMOS   You can't do that!

LANA   Who says?!

TOMOS   I DO!!!

LANA   Help me choose then. I don't really care.

TOMOS   Enid.

LANA   Okay, she's Enid. That's suitably dull.

TOMOS   And I like Marvin. Well, I don't actually like it, but I think it fits.

LANA   And I agree. All right, he's Marvin. Enid and Marvin. Delightfully gruesome.

TOMOS   You know, I have to tell you, sometimes it's a lot of fun trying to keep up with you.

LANA   I'm unpredictable, you like that.

TOMOS   It's true.

# INTERMISSION

<u>ACT THREE</u>

# ACT THREE, SCENE ONE

LANA    So – after a brief musical introduction with much
        tail-coated white-cuffed arm waving, we find
        Enid and Marvin, Marvin and Enid inside a hired
        vehicle, a rented car – she says hire, he says rent.

TOMOS   *Let's call the whole thing off!*

LANA    In fact, it is the thin-thinner-thinnest end of a
        colossal cultural wedge.

TOMOS   Oh yeah, right. That would come up, I suppose.

LANA    It's the tip of an iceberg.

TOMOS   Really? Well, it's good to be reminded that this is a
        tragedy. The looming–

LANA    May I continue? Though she, Enid, is capable of
        being extraordinarily bold, she–

TOMOS   –Example?

LANA    Of her boldness? Not now. I'll think of one later.

TOMOS   I make note.

LANA    Thank you. I do not know if this can be
        successfully presented on stage or not but
        here goes. Though Enid is capable of being
        extraordinarily bold, she chooses this moment not
        to be. She has done her fair share of dicing with
        death for the sheer thrill of it, especially behind
        the wheel of a car.

— 89 —

TOMOS   She's a closet daredevil.

LANA   Indeed – and the closet has no door, I should add.

TOMOS   An alcove daredevil.

LANA   Oh very funny, where was I? Ah yes, listen carefully: first option: steering wheel on the right side of the vehicle, vehicle driven on the left side of the road, this she has learned, knows, and therefore prefers.

TOMOS   As in the United Kingdom.

LANA   Correct. Her *country of origin*.

TOMOS   Australia too, I think.

LANA   Are you sure?

TOMOS   No!

LANA   Second option: That most dangerous and challenging of arrangements for any driver – steering wheel on right side of vehicle, vehicle driven on right side of road – this she has not learned but is in fact familiar with, though definitely does *not* prefer. Familiar with because, for the duration of a certain period of her life, this driving arrangement was experienced by her on a daily basis.....

TOMOS   She has lived on the continent?

LANA   Yes. She lived for a few years in Germany but drove a right-hand-drive car during that time.

TOMOS   Hmm. That would be a bit of a challenge.

— 90 —

LANA     Only one other combination remains: steering
         wheel on left side of vehicle, vehicle driven on
         right side of road. This arrangement she has not
         in fact experienced but is familiar with, having
         encountered it, visually – in films. She is a little
         apprehensive about it. Since she is aware that it is
         the one arrangement that he knows best, perhaps
         the only one he knows, she decides, *Why not let
         him drive?* Whisper to her that, in due course,
         this arrangement will represent the norm and she
         would laugh immoderately, incredulously....while
         toying with the idea of its materialisation.

TOMOS    *In due course.*

LANA     Right.

TOMOS    But how long is that? Days? Months? Years?

LANA     Months, less than a year.

TOMOS    Say that then, it has a better ring to it: *Less than a
         year.*

LANA     Okay, no problem. Shall I repeat?

TOMOS    Yes, let's hear it.

LANA     Whisper to her that, in less than a year, this
         arrangement will represent the norm, the
         status quo, and she would laugh immoderately,
         incredulously, while toying with the idea of its
         materialisation.

TOMOS    Perfect.

*END OF ACT THREE, SCENE ONE*

TOMOS   We are getting along better now, aren't we?

LANA    Yes.

TOMOS   Though of course I'm the one who has to actually say it. You wouldn't dream of saying it, would you?

LANA    I have other qualities, remember?

TOMOS   Yeah, yeah. Like winning a medal for beating about the bush.

LANA    Too kind.

## ACT THREE, SCENE TWO

LANA So here is our new scene at last. The set is reduced to the interior of a smallish car which he drives. The car has been named after a horse. They talk. The lies on her side of the conversation continue but now they are lies she actually believes because she wants him to want her, and we sympathise with this common female failing – well, some do, other are disgusted or even appalled by it, they are the ones who have not thoroughly studied the programme wherein the year of the original production is given, 1979, i.e. post-Woodstock, pre-post-modern, token feminism, men still on top.

TOMOS Like what exactly?

LANA Mm?

TOMOS What are the lies that she believes – one will do.

LANA That her usual state is calm and collected.

TOMOS Really?

LANA She is when she wants to be – but in fact this is an erroneus label.

TOMOS I don't understand.

LANA She likes to appear calm and collected sometimes, but in fact it is merely passivity.

TOMOS Okay. One more?

LANA That she needs a man.

— 93 —

TOMOS  Better. They will like that much better.

LANA  Well – it *is* the late seventies. The issue of whether
she wants him is of no importance, it is not a
feature of the game. She has been brainwashed
into believing that she must have a male, that the
ultimate goal of a woman is to be part of a couple.
So every candidate must be considered. Her
personal requirements in this arena have not been
defined. She plunges into the wilderness. It is a
function of her femaleness to call into the wild and
wait for a response from a male. It is expected. It is
necessary. It is conditioned. It is horrible.

TOMOS  You don't think this will come across as the
author's message?

LANA  Oh – it's not too terribly obvious, is it?

TOMOS  Not *too* terribly, no.

LANA  I'll ignore that little dig. Where was I? Being
young – ish, attractive, and possibly–

TOMOS  I'm sorry but can I stop you for a moment? You'll
probably hate me for this but could we have a
reminder of what they look like – you know,
the usual stuff? – I know you've already mostly
covered it but I'm not sure I've retained it all and
I actually don't think you have mentioned how
old they are. Do you mind? Paint me a picture of
them, would you? D'you mind?

LANA  Very well. Enid is twenty-nine years old, she is
five feet three inches tall, she has red hair – dyed
– and grey eyes. She is British. Marvin is twenty-

six years old, he is five feet ten inches tall, he weighs one hundred and twenty pounds, he has dark brown hair and brown eyes. He is American. Okay?

TOMOS   Five ten and a hundred and twenty pounds.... My god, he's a rake!

LANA   I was not exaggerating. Now, where was I?

TOMOS   You were analysing the reason for her lying.

LANA   I was? And I thought I was being – deep.

TOMOS   ...?

LANA   Joke. Enid: being young – ish, attractive and available, though this has yet to be confirmed, means there is actually no need for her to lie.... if only she knew that she does not have to lie; in fact, if she but knew it, a confession of her imperfections to this man would only increase her allure. *To this man* – very important. Except that the imperfections she has are not the ones she thinks she has and some instinct in her knows this. The egotistical but insecure male cannot tolerate contradiction from a woman, so were she to deny her beauty, her intelligence, her wit, he would stop listening. Let us be kind and say that, instead of lying about what she regards as shortcomings in her character, she – skirts around them. Waltzes around them in fact.

TOMOS   That's all very psychological, you know.

LANA   Yes, well we are coming back to the physical again now.

— 95 —

TOMOS   Good.

LANA   The stage lights redden indicating that warmth is
increasing within the car. The landscape they drive
through has been chilled–

TOMOS   Where are they again?

LANA   In a northern state. The landscape has been chilled
by a fall of snow, the already muted colours are
bleached pale and the sky is white with cloud,
but their immediate environment – the interior
of the car – is the colour of blood, the red-orange
fluid which courses through their bodies. There
is absolutely no doubt that these two will have sex
before dawn. The question – the only question – is
where will this occur, her room or his? The chill
outside the car is the chill of harsh reality but their
warmth keeps it at bay and will continue to do
so....for how long, we do not know, but not for
ever, we may know that.

TOMOS   A tragedy, as you have been saying all along.

LANA   Heat – that amazing phenomenon, the generation
of heat in the human body – where essentially no
heat exists – produced by the muscled engine of
the heart. Blast, I forgot to describe the hands.

TOMOS   No you didn't.

LANA   I did.

TOMOS   You said she had the hands of a milkmaid!

LANA   But I didn't describe his hands, I only talked about

— 96 —

where they had been on her body. So, let's see –
while she has the hands of a hoyden, he–

TOMOS   A what?

LANA    It's another word for milkmaid, a type of
milkmaid.

TOMOS   Are you having me on?

LANA    Only a little. She has the hands of a hoyden, he has
the hands of a libidinant.

TOMOS   What is that exactly?

LANA    There is a dictionary over on that shelf. His hands–

TOMOS   Never mind. I think I can guess.

LANA    His hands: palms elongated north to south, fingers
long and tapering, rising, when assembled, like
the façade of a Gothic cathedral, solid at the base,
diminishing with height, nails squared, thumb
acutely curved. Skin pale, smooth, relatively
unlined. These are the hands of a man who is
a stranger to hard physical labour. The person
to whom these hands belong dislikes excess, is
incisive, cold, egotistical, pompous, probably a
perfectionist, but highly sexual....gluttonously
sexual.

TOMOS   Wow, that's quite an assumption. You couldn't
possibly tell all that from his hands alone.

LANA    It's not as assumption, it's an assertion.

TOMOS   They won't know that.

— 97 —

LANA    They?

TOMOS   The audience. Or had you forgotten them – again?

LANA    Her palms are broader than they are long, fingers
        radiate in an arc from the upper edge of the palm,
        a hint of deformity in the ring finger as it cleaves
        towards the middle finger of each hand; there is art
        there, but there is also labour.

TOMOS   What about projecting a picture of their hands
        onto a backdrop?

LANA    Fine.

TOMOS   That's all you can say – fine?

LANA    I am more concerned with the music. As the lights
        redden, the music must be – relentless, repetitive,
        monotone....Glassesque. Quick, the red towel,
        the colour of the fluid oozing from her lowest
        orifice (when she is standing or sitting) as the
        unimpregnated vessel contained within her pelvic
        cavity sloughs offs its uselessly blooded lining. She
        spreads the red towel across the white sheet of his
        bed.

TOMOS   His bed – but they are in the car!

LANA    A transition then. We will do what you suggest....
        some kind of close-up of their hands, individually
        then together, as an interlude between these
        two scenes, with the lights reddening and the
        maddening tension of the music mounting still
        further.

— 98 —

TOMOS   I've got it.

LANA    What?

TOMOS   Project images of their hands onto the back wall,
        then other parts of their bodies as they – you know
        – get it on. First with clothes on – a shoulder, a
        hand, a thigh, the bulge in his pants, a kind of
        collage of body parts with romantic overtones, all
        pulled together with lights and sound – then with
        their clothes coming off – and – and –

LANA    With the lights getting redder and redder until the
        red is the red of the towel she is spreading across
        the bed. Yes!

TOMOS   Like in a movie!

LANA    As in a movie, *please*.

TOMOS   Whatever.

LANA    But I do like it.

TOMOS   I can see that.

LANA    So back to the bed in the corner of the stage.

TOMOS   No! *Centre* stage.

*END OF ACT THREE, SCENE TWO*

# ACT THREE, SCENE THREE

LANA — He laughs insensitively at her delicacy, her concern for, her – consideration of – others.... while taking advantage of it. This motif will recur strongly and in other keys, minor and major.

TOMOS — I don't understand.

LANA — This concern of hers for the feelings of other sentient beings has enormous potential, as does his insensitivity. The tips of two more icebergs. What don't you understand?

TOMOS — Other keys, minor and major.

LANA — Another attempt on my part to be poetic, I suppose.

TOMOS — You're really a poet, aren't you?

LANA — It's how I started out.

TOMOS — So it has no real meaning, it just sounds pretty?

LANA — ...That's a little harsh....but, yes, that's about it. The less romantically inclined members of the audience will already have made a mental note of this schism, this divide, this – incipient incompatibility. Those more firmly in the grip of their collective conditioning for romance, stubbornly continue to hope for that happy ending – that white dress – that ring – those bells... But sometimes a short sharp shock is more effective than persuasion. A relationship follows–

TOMOS   What was that about a short sharp shock? Did I
        miss something?

LANA    Just listen and be patient, it's coming. A
        relationship follows rogering and romance –
        everyone knows that....but the myth of endurance
        – no amount of alliteration will topple that. The
        power to push this story uphill is not what is
        required, rather the need is for brakes to impede
        its hastening downhill. The thing will sail down
        almost of its own accord.

TOMOS   Meaning?

LANA    Meaning the two oldest clichés of human
        communion: the need of the male to establish at
        his side a suitable mate available for fucking at any
        time of day or night and the drive of the female to
        be reinforced in her womanhood by the production
        of offspring, an act which necessitates the
        protection of the male – two very different aims,
        you must admit.

TOMOS   Must I?

LANA    Yes!!!

*END OF ACT THREE, SCENE THREE*

TOMOS   Times have changed, you know.

LANA    You keep forgetting, this is the seventies.

TOMOS   I'm tired.

LANA    Let us talk a little about society, about social
        mores, habits, customs, that kind of thing. In
        short, let us indulge in a little gossip.

TOMOS   At last – dialogue.

LANA    I knew that would make you perk up.

## ACT THREE, SCENE FOUR

LANA      Two bulky sour-faced women, Gladys and Lillian, waddle onto the stage. Both have skin the colour and texture of uncooked pastry, each wears a shapeless overcoat and dated hat, carries a large old-fashioned handbag plus a full shopping bag. They begin to converse in strong regional accents:

Glad: Oh 'ello, Lil, 'ow are you?

Lil:     O....fair to middlin' like. Can't complain, Glad. Fair to middlin'. And 'ow are you, luv?

Glad: Can't complain. Wouldn' do any good, if we did, would it?

Lil:     Tha's right. Not a bit o' good. Grin and bear it. So wha's this I 'ear about Enid then?

Glad: She's met this chap in America.

Lil:     I knew *somethin'* was goin' on.

Glad: She's livin' with somebody else, yew know tha', don't yew?

Lil:     That chap in London? Aye, I knew. 'e doesn't count though, and anyway, 'e sleeps with other women.

Glad: But she's just spongin' off 'im?

Lil:     'e doesn' mind, mun!

Glad: 'e doesn' know!!

Lil:     Course 'e does. But 'e thinks 'e's winnin' 'er

— 103 —

over. So 'e pays for everything and she lets 'im.

Glad: Does 'e indeed!

Lil: 'e thinks they 'ave a future together. 'e wants to get married, but she 'as no intention of marryin' 'im. She's just usin' 'im.

Glad: She's still married to 'er first 'usband!

Lil: No, they're gettin' a divorce, mun.

Glad: Look, oo's side are yew on?

Lil: Nobody's. I'm just statin' facts, tha's all.

Glad: Facts. I'll give you a fact. She's gettin' ready to run off with this new fella soon as yew like.

Lil: And what about this new fella?

Glad: What about 'im?

Lil: 'e's divorced.

Glad: When?

Lil: Six months ago. Nearly killed 'im, it did. 'e's got a temper, that's what I 'eard.

Glad: 'oo told 'ew that then?

Lil: A little bird.

Glad: Everybody's got a temper.

Lil: Put 'is fist through a window, tha's what I 'eard. Tha's why 'is first wife left 'im.

Glad: She was probably to blame. Yew know 'ow

— 104 —

infuriatin' some women are.

Lil: Oo's side are yew on?

Glad: I'm just statin' facts, tha's all, just like somebody else was a minute ago.

Lil: Very funny, I don't think.

Glad: Enid isn' bein' honest with this new chap.

Lil: Neither is 'e with 'er!

Glad: She 'asn' even mentioned this man in London to 'im.

Lil: Why should she? 'e 'asn' mentioned 'is girlfriend neither.

Glad: Girlfriend?

Lil: Someone 'e met on the rebound.

Glad: Well, I dunno about tha', but all I'm sayin' is this, she's not sayin' anything about the chap in London tha's all I know. Seems to me she's livin' with one, draggin' one be'ind 'er in the dust and now she's got 'er eye on a third. She's still married, yew know, and she 'as no job, no money, never thinks about the future.

Lil: She'll get money from the divorce, mun.

Glad: This new chap will think 'e's struck gold!

Lil: In a way 'e 'as. She isn' much of a planner though. She'll just fritter it all away in no time. No ambition, tha's 'er trouble.

Glad: I don' think tha's the right word for it, really.

— 105 —

Lil:    What then?

Glad   O, I dunno why we are bein' so silly about all this. Nobody 'as any control over wha's about to 'appen.

Lil:    Be nice if we 'ad a crystal ball.

Glad:   Fat lot of good that would do.

Lil:    No, I s'pose not. Come on in for bit, I'll put the kettle on, I could do with a cuppa.

Glad:   Aye, tha'd be nice.

TOMOS   That was fun! But I'm not sure what I was supposed to understand...

LANA    He's violent and she's aimless: it's a perfect match.

*END OF ACT THREE, SCENE FOUR*

TOMOS    Where's the white shirt with the unbuttoned cuff?

LANA     It's coming, it's coming...

TOMOS    What about some more dialogue?

LANA     Dialogue, dialogue, is that all you can think
         about?!

TOMOS    Well, excuse me!

LANA     I'm sorry, I apologise. After all, What is the use of
         a book without conversation?

TOMOS    I didn't say that.

LANA     It's a quote, from *Alice In Wonderland*.

TOMOS    Oh.

LANA     One learns something new every day. You want
         them to have a conversation, is that it? Enid and
         Marvin?

TOMOS    Please.

LANA     Hmmm. I knew this would come up.

TOMOS    The usual, you know, how old are you, when's
         your birthday, where are you from, what do you
         do for a living, where do you live, do you smoke,
         do you drink, do you do drugs, are you going out
         with anyone, do you have kids, have you ever been
         married, do you have any brothers and sisters, are
         your parents still alive, do you have a car....what
         do you eat for breakfast.

LANA     What do you eat for breakfast? Oh, surely not.

— 107 —

TOMOS   Why not?

LANA    That's like saying – let's spend the night together.
        The things people say these days.

TOMOS   Well, perhaps not your generation.

LANA    How the hell old do you think I am?

TOMOS   Ninety-two?

LANA    Don't be facetious.

TOMOS   Look, I was joking. I know how old you are. I also
        know you had a very sheltered upbringing, you're
        naïve.

LANA    It's true, I am naïve.

TOMOS   It's touching.

LANA    I can't help it.

TOMOS   Let's have some naïve dialogue then.

LANA    You mean how old are you, where are you from,
        what do you do for a living, when's your birthday,
        where do you live, do you smoke, do you drink, do
        you do drugs, are you going out with anyone, do
        you have children, have you ever been married, do
        you have any brothers and sisters, are your parents
        still alive, do you have a car....what do you eat for
        breakfast, or should I say, what are you like in
        bed?

TOMOS   With *answers!*

LANA    No, I can't do it.

— 108 —

TOMOS  You will regret this.

LANA  I want to get to the next thing on the list.

TOMOS  And what's that?

LANA  The bus journey.

TOMOS  The bus journey....okay, that's good. Bus journeys are good, they are kind of – romantic. And they could have their conversation on the bus.

LANA  I can't.

TOMOS  What do you mean, you can't?

LANA  I can't go on.

TOMOS  Now what!?!

LANA  It's a quotation.

TOMOS  I'm not interested in your quotations! Get on with the story, will you!

LANA  Screw the story. What am I – an entertainer?

TOMOS  Yes. Amongst other things.

LANA  Amongst – other – things?

TOMOS  Entertain the idea that you are an entertainer.

LANA  Do not try to be clever, it does not suit you.

TOMOS  Don't have a go at me, I'm not the problem.

LANA  Oh, and I am?

TOMOS  You are the problem, yes. You are also the solution.

— 109 —

LANA    Christ, don't start analysing me or we'll be here till the cows come home.

TOMOS   The cows have *come* home! Now it's time to count them and milk them.

LANA    What is that supposed to mean?! Anyway, I thought you were tired!

TOMOS   *Please, I beg you.* Be so good as to continue. Say what you have to say.

LANA    ...

TOMOS   Are you crying?

LANA    Yes.

TOMOS   Then cry.

LANA    Will you hold me for a moment?

TOMOS   What?

LANA    Please.

TOMOS   Okay, okay. [*Embraces* LANA]....is that better?

LANA    Yes. Thank you. I'm okay now, you can let go.

TOMOS   [*Releases her*] What made you start crying?

LANA    You – you were being kind.

TOMOS   Kindness is very important.

LANA    A little goes a long way.

TOMOS   Then....be so kind....as to continue. Begin by being

— 110 —

kind to yourself.

LANA  No critical study, however brilliant, is the fierce psychological battle a novel is.

TOMOS  I'm sure that's true.

LANA  It's a quotation.

TOMOS  No. More. Quotations. I *mean* it. Go on with the story.

LANA  Who are you anyway?

TOMOS  You know who I am.

LANA  Do I?

TOMOS  Keep....going.

LANA  Could I have a cup of tea?

TOMOS  Of course. If you think it will help.

LANA  Nice and strong. Milk, no sugar.

TOMOS  I'll be back in a few minutes. Keep going. [*Exits*]

LANA  ...Alone....at last....I want to look back but I dare not – no – that's not it. There's not much I wouldn't dare....in the security of my own mind. I want to see if I can resist the temptation to look back before going on – no, still not it. I want to try and deny myself the – the – the luxury of looking back. Why am I so stern with my own mind? That's easily answered – I still don't know how to play. Oh stop, you're breaking my heart. Where was I? The wedding – how about that?

— 111 —

God! No! I know, I'll throw in an intermission –
yes. Time for the audience to raise their flattened
behinds from the thin scratchy wine-coloured
plush of their seats and suspend their suspension
of disbelief (if that is what they have been doing).
Hundreds of bodies surge into various other areas
of the building, areas which have stood hushed
and tomblike while the action has been going on
in the auditorium, areas where the voices on stage
have resounded and echoed like those of ghosts
from a more distant tomb. They are in search
of refreshment. The balcony bar for example,
aptly called the Crush bar, fills up with humans
buzzing with the desire for drinks and discussion
and the need for display. There is much looking
without seeing....ah, that aloof stare of those who
are much more aware of being seen than seeing.
Some patrons disguise their selfconsciousness with
all kinds of fascinating nervous tics while some
display scorn....as if it were a kind of currency
they have successfully accumulated while others
have not. Bar staff, unabashed but reserved,
bend a condescending ear to hear the orders for
drinks, then turn their backs to pour liquids of
dizzying variety and consistency into glasses of
equally various shapes, sizes and thicknesses,
then turn again to place these concoctions on a
polished wood surface protected by rectangular
bar towels bearing garish adverts, before receiving
the appropriate pieces of paper and discs of metal
in their extended palms and turning again to
deposit the money into the till. Then they turn
back to help the next customer. These bartenders

spend the whole interval turning and returning towards and away from the two surfaces. To their customers whom they call patrons they whisper or proclaim – depending on their personality – the prices of the drinks requested. There is much sipping and swallowing of fluids, much fingering, grasping, turning and handling of glassware, and a great deal of elevated – if in volume only – conversation: *What do you think of the show so far?* The intensity of this question is often dependent upon – even a function of – the attitude of the person who arranged the event, who *dressed* for the event, or who decided on the event in the first place (though the early stages of a relationship – *the sex is so good* – exert an influence...) or, perhaps, it's a case of *Darling, they are singing our song.* Or not. Other possible comments: *It's a bit disjointed, don't you think? He's a bit of a weed, don't you think? She's so weak, don't you think, so insecure.* Audiences love to watch themselves when they are not watching the show. This interval production is often more interesting than the production it bifurcates. (*You think so?*) And then what? The fourth act....watched through the haze created by mild drunkenness. It had better be good if it is going to hold their attention...

**INTERMISSION**

ACT FOUR

# ACT FOUR, SCENE ONE

TOMOS  Here's your tea. Wake up, the audience is coming back!

LANA  I wasn't asleep. They are suddenly part of–

TOMOS  They? Who? Here's your tea.

LANA  You know who!

TOMOS  You mean Enid and Marvin?

LANA  Yes!

TOMOS  But how does the audience know that?

LANA  There they are!

TOMOS  Where?!

LANA  There! On stage! The audience can see them!! Now can I begin?

TOMOS  Go ahead. I'll murder you later.

LANA  Their individual journeys merge into a joint journey. He has persuaded her to stay in the country longer than she has planned or can afford. The instant she decides this she wires a friend back home asking for financial support. He provides it without question. When that money runs out she knows she must return.

TOMOS  Is that the guy she is living with in London?

— 117 —

LANA      Yes.

TOMOS    Has she told him about Marvin?

LANA      Not in so many words. Along with other people
          she has encountered on her journey, Marvin has
          been mentioned in her correspondence, though
          not by name.

TOMOS    What's the name of the guy in London?

LANA      Bernard.

TOMOS    And does Bernard – suspect anything?

LANA      You mean, that he may be about to be usurped?

TOMOS    If that's how you want to put it.

LANA      Yes, he does. But he is not allowing this suspicion
          to interrupt his regular and successful search for
          female....companionship.

TOMOS    He is screwing around while she's gone.

LANA      Correct.

TOMOS    And he assumes that Enid is also screwing around.

LANA      Correct. May I continue? Enid and Marvin are
          suddenly part of the shifting population of a long-
          distance Greyhound bus. Their individual journeys
          have merged into one journey and they are about
          to cover a lot of ground, literally and figuratively.
          The low-class sordid atmosphere of the bus adds
          an aura of romance to their commingling. Odd
          that, how squalour tugs at the heart even as it
          disgusts. They do not belong here, yet here they

— 118 —

are. What is Enid's opinion of these beings, these foreign creatures? This is the clearest her vision of them will ever be, it is childlike because she is undeveloped, tragically undeveloped. She has the freshness and vulnerability of a blooming rose – also a few thorns.

*END OF ACT FOUR, SCENE ONE*

LANA    You're very quiet.

TOMOS   How's your tea?

LANA    Mmm, perfect. ...I said, you're very quiet.

TOMOS   I have decided to be more sparing with my comments.

LANA    As long as you are not suppressing anything.

TOMOS   I can't promise that.

LANA    I was going to talk more about thorns. Do you think the audience would like that?

TOMOS   You mean thorns as a metaphor.

LANA    Well – yes.

TOMOS   Not necessary. Go on with the story.

LANA    Let's glance back for a moment.

TOMOS   Backwards – again.

LANA    It's relevant! I thought you were going to be more sparing with comments.

TOMOS   Sorry! It's just that – no, go ahead, please, say what you have to say.

## ACT FOUR, SCENE TWO

LANA    In the course of fucking her that first time he
said to her, *I didn't know you'd be so sensitive.* He
probably means her lack of utterance – she is silent
during sexual intercourse. There is a reason for
this. There is a man, a distant cousin of hers, still
living though now very elderly, who established
in her this mute acceptance of advances she would
prefer not to receive and even those she willingly
accepts. She has no memory of this part of her
education; it was successfully blocked deep within
her psyche at a level a fraction more profound
than the horror of it. But the ensuing nightmares
and her refusal to eat were good indications of the
depth of this horror. For almost a week after the
incident she refused all food and for a prolonged
period after that would consume only a smear
of a salty brown spread on thin buttered toast.
Fortunately the spread was rich in B vitamins.

TOMOS   Do you mean – Marmite?

LANA    Yes.

TOMOS   Well, that should evoke a response, people either
love or hate that stuff.

LANA    What about you?

TOMOS   Oh, I love it.

LANA    Me too. I mean, so do I.

TOMOS   So does my cat!

— 121 —

LANA    You think I should actually use the name?
        Marmite?

TOMOS   Nah, let them work it out for themselves. Go on,
        this is interesting. Are you going to show that early
        – damage?

LANA    No. I mean, not at this moment. Anything else
        would be unbearable.

TOMOS   Unbearable? Who for?

LANA    For whom – *please*. For me.

TOMOS   But how are they going to understa–

LANA    It will be revealed later, when I can – when I can
        face recalling it. For now we see the family sitting
        down to eat and her pushing her plate away.

TOMOS   But you will get round to it?

LANA    Absolutely. So – there were various tests
        conducted in an attempt to ascertain the cause of
        this abrupt cessation of ingestion.

TOMOS   W-h-a-a-t?

LANA    Tests. To find out why she does not eat.

TOMOS   You know, there are times when I could kick you.

LANA    Feel free.

TOMOS   No, I'll get someone else to do it, I don't want your
        blood on my hands.

LANA    There were visits to the family doctor, she was

— 122 —

subjected to physiological and psychological tests, all with inconclusive results. The one she remembers is the electroencephalogram – for that test it was necessary that a clear sticky jelly be applied to her scalp to ensure good conductivity.

TOMOS Is that like a – a brain test?

LANA Yes. The one where thin scratchy pen-nibs get pulled across a strip of paper and leave wiggly lines. She watched that happen. Wires were attached to her head and she sat and watched the narrow strip of paper, rolling out of the machine, telling the doctors about what was going on inside her head... [bitter]....as if anything could. The paper had very thin red vertical lines on it and the wiggly lines were black and horizontal – well, they jumped around of course, to show she was still alive and her brain was functioning, but they were basically horizontal.

TOMOS Do they still do that? It sounds pretty quaint.

LANA I doubt it. But it was certainly the case in the early sixties.

TOMOS That would make a good backdrop, don't you think?

LANA` Backdrop?

TOMOS The squiggly black lines, moving across a strip of white paper – with thin red vertical lines.

LANA I like that.

— 123 —

TOMOS   People love stuff about the brain. Hey, I've got
it. Let's have another banner emerging from the
wings carried by stage hands – the strip of paper –
the lines – the red, the black. Can't you see it?

LANA    We'll do it.

TOMOS   We?

LANA    We're a team, aren't we?

TOMOS   Are we?

LANA    Of course. What happened to your resolution?

TOMOS   Yeah, yeah. So what was going on inside her head?

LANA    A process of numbing, the numbing of the horror
and pain of what the distant cousin had done....a
process which did not appear in the results of the
test.

TOMOS   She was traumatised.

LANA    Correct. The sticky jelly was vigorously shampooed
out of her hair by her mother and eventually the
demands of her child's growing body–

TOMOS   How old was she, did we say?

LANA    We?

TOMOS   You said we were a team!

LANA    Just kidding, of course we're a team. No, it wasn't
mentioned. She is six years old. Where was I?
– the demands of her growing body eventually
conquer her inability to accept larger quantities

— 124 —

of food but the nightmares – the nightmares will continue for the rest of her life though the intervals between their occurrence will lengthen.

TOMOS  Are you going to tell us what the nightmares are?

LANA  There is only one – that her tongue is too big for her mouth. 'nough said?

TOMOS  You mean–

LANA  Precisely.

TOMOS  Men are such bastards. Wow. Imagine showing that on stage.

LANA  I intend to.

TOMOS  You are? Well, I think you need to prepare them – give them some time here – to absorb *that* gruesome piece of information.

*END OF ACT FOUR, SCENE TWO*

LANA    Well, something has to happen meanwhile. What do you suggest?

TOMOS  Another musical interlude, perhaps?

LANA    Hmmmm....what about a poem?

TOMOS  Why not both?

LANA    I've got it! You'll like this.

## ACT FOUR, SCENE THREE

LANA    The stage is filled with young girls, shoulder to
shoulder – no, holding hands, all holding hands,
but higgledy-piggledy all over the stage, not in
straight lines. They enter joyfully, laughing,
singing, giggling, humming, chanting, smiling –
the energy is one hundred percent positive. They
fill the stage, spiralling around a central point, so
that the people in the upper circle get the full effect
of this – this whirlpool of girlhood.

TOMOS  That's great! – a whirlpo–

LANA    Don't interrupt! Round and round they go, still
making their various joyful sounds until – until –
until!....aaargh! Lights down! Fade to black!

*END OF ACT FOUR, SCENE THREE*

LANA    I'm stuck. Help me.

TOMOS   Stuck?

LANA    I don't know what should happen next.

TOMOS   Well, what are you trying to say? What's your
        point?

LANA    I haven't got a point!

TOMOS   Of course you have. It's about the nightmare – you
        are explaining the nightmare.

LANA    But I don't want to explain it!

TOMOS   But you said you would – you were doing so well!

LANA    I – I – I –

TOMOS   You want to make the point that Enid was sexually
        abused as a child, yes?

LANA    I've already made that point.

TOMOS   You alluded to it, that's all.

LANA    But that's my thing, alluding...

TOMOS   But sometimes you have to be more – direct. More
        clear. Look, remember that section where you had
        the stage full of male stereotypes, guys who had
        *entered her cavity.*

LANA    Yes.

TOMOS   Well, it's a bit like that. A way of depicting it
        visually.

— 128 —

LANA      Is it?

TOMOS    They'll love it – colour and movement – go on, you
         can do it.

LANA      Girlwood....that's what I'm getting at.

TOMOS    What?

LANA      I read it in a poem somewhere it's very graphic,
         very moving. I just can't remember who wrote
         it....the poet was sexually abused as a girl. Linda...

TOMOS    It wasn't you?

LANA      No! Linda somebody or other.

TOMOS    What was it again?

LANA      Girlwood....green girlwood. *He splits the green
         girlwood of her body.*

TOMOS    My god, that's graphic....I know – dress them in
         green!

LANA      Who?

TOMOS    The little girls on stage. Dress them in green!

LANA      Yes, that's it! Oh, thank you, thank you, thank
         you.

TOMOS    My pleasure.

## ACT FOUR, SCENE FOUR

LANA   There they are, this mass of little girls, hand in
hand, spiralling, in their green dresses – and we'll
have either a voice reciting the poem or else have
the words projected onto the back wall of the
stage – or both! When the voice and the projected
words reach that phrase –*he splits the green girlwood
of her body* – suddenly the crowd of girls splits
straight down the middle – it will have to be very
stringently choreographed – and each half runs
off, *screaming.*

TOMOS   That should make 'em sit up.

LANA   You think? Okay, I'll work the details out later.
End of that scene. [*Sigh of relief*] What *is* that
woman's name?

*END OF ACT FOUR, SCENE FOUR*

TOMOS   That's the first time you've smiled since the
        intermission.

LANA    I'm sorry, I'm exhausted.

TOMOS   You don't have to apologise. I can see how
        important this is to you.

LANA    Can you?

TOMOS   Of course.

LANA    It's the only thing that gives my life meaning. It's
        awful really, but that's the truth. Ah well....now
        for him....next scene – I've completely lost count –
        what is it?

TOMOS   Just tell the story. There will be ups and downs but
        you will get there in the end. Just keep going.

LANA    You're so encouraging. If you only knew what it
        means to me to hear someone say those words.

TOMOS   That's what I'm here for. Now – him.

LANA    I am so lucky, to have you.

TOMOS   I'm glad to hear it. Get back to describing him.

LANA    I lov–

TOMOS   Don't say it!

LANA    No. All right....I've just remembered – who wrote
        it, the green girlwood poem. Linda McCarriston.

## ACT FOUR, SCENE FIVE

LANA    Marvin, too, suffers from nightmares. Or perhaps they are simply bad dreams.

TOMOS   Is there a difference?

LANA    I think so. Let us say nightmares, for the symmetry. Whatever they are, they are of the classic male frustration type, frustration fuelled to intolerable levels by the actions of a callous insensitive male parent with whom the boy never bonded and by whom the boy was regularly beaten. In his sleep, the boy fights – but never once gets the better of – his father. In his other dreams, he happily fucks his mother and his younger sister. Given the opportunity and the licence, he also would do so in his waking life. He craves their slender thighs, moist hairy cunts, slim torsos, and large plump rounded breasts. He slides his hand between his mother's thighs, he fondles his sister's breast, he rubs himself against her firm rump. Perhaps the rage and the desire are equal – or is that an oversimplification?

TOMOS   I was just wondering how you would show all that on stage...

LANA    Pretty straightforwardly, I think.

TOMOS   A boy fucking his mother?!

LANA    I take your point. Hmmm... I have it – okay, please listen carefully because I am going to say a lot of things in a short space of time and I may overlook

— 132 —

something and then forget to go back and insert it.

TOMOS  I could use a recorder.

LANA  You have one?

TOMOS  A little handheld thing. I've got it here somewhere, wait a minute....yeah, here it is.

LANA  Why didn't you mention it before?

TOMOS  I don't know.

LANA  You could have mentioned it before. It might have saved a lot of time, you know.

TOMOS  I wasn't sure you'd want me to use it. Get back to the–

LANA  You only had to ask.

TOMOS  Yes, that's true, but I didn't. Go on with–

LANA  Why not?

TOMOS  Perhaps I was a bit nervous about asking. Continue with–

LANA  Are you really that afraid of me?

TOMOS  [*Cornered*] Perhaps, yes.

LANA  [*Incredulous*] *You're afraid of me?*

TOMOS  A little. Is that so hard to believe?

LANA  I'm crushed.

TOMOS  Well don't be. It's the other side of respect, think

— 133 —

of it that way.

LANA   The other side of....is that really it? Respect?

TOMOS  Yes.

LANA   [*Recovering*] All right, here goes: three beds on stage, single, double, single, all pushed together downstage centre, heads of the bed upstage. In the outlying single beds Marvin and Enid lie asleep, uncovered. They roll over onto the double bed, still asleep but now side by side. They begin to dream, twitches, mutterings, muscle spasms, gasps, as their respective nightmares begin. Enid whimpers, Marvin kicks out. They roll apart again into their single beds. He becomes more agitated, he thrashes about, while she becomes rigid, her breathing shallow and rapid. She covers her mouth with both hands and shakes her head from side to side. He rolls onto his stomach and starts to hump the mattress. Two actors, one representing Marvin, one Enid, enter from the wings. They are followed by other actors representing the other parties in these nightmares. The aforementioned unspeakable acts occur, executed as graphically as possible, considering the extent of the unspeakability. Enid and Marvin sleep on, tortured by their nightmares, while we see what is going on inside their heads, enacted on either side.

*END OF ACT FOUR, SCENE FIVE*

TOMOS   That will take a little working out.

LANA    That's the general idea anyway.

TOMOS   So we see Marvin, as a young boy, taunted by his father?

LANA    To an extreme.

TOMOS   Then we see him as he fucks his mother and sister?

LANA    Yes.

TOMOS   And Enid, as a young girl, a man she trusts sticks his cock into her mouth.

LANA    Yes. You can turn that thing off now.

TOMOS   Well, I'll say this. It makes a pretty strong statement theatrically.

LANA    That's my aim. Ergo–

TOMOS   What does that mean exactly? I've always wondered.

LANA    Look it up. Ergo: she is infected with the knowledge of what it feels like to put her trust in another, to be desired – though she may not fully understand this yet–

TOMOS   She probably knows what it is to be pleasing – to be pleasing to grown-ups.

LANA    Yes – where was I?....infected with knowledge – no – rather....experience. She is infected with the experience of what it feels like to put her trust in another, then be an object of pleasure, be pawed

— 135 —

and fondled, then deflowered either physically
or psychologically or both, and left numb. These
words are not available to her – she can barely read
– all she knows is feelings, instinct. The words are
labels that will be applied later when her intellect
develops. This experience, this introduction to
being the vehicle for a man's satisfaction – this
ghastly baptism – is a very common disease, one of
epidemic proportions but this does not diminish its
profound and tragically far-reaching effects on the
individual abused.

TOMOS   And not just girls either.

LANA   Absolutely not. Just think of the priesthood.

TOMOS   You're on form today.

LANA   Am I? Now we have to get him in the picture.
Damn, I used 'ergo' too soon.

TOMOS   Good. I haven't looked it up yet.

LANA   While he is infected with the cross-contamination
of rage and lasciviousness – forget the ergo – it's
just a fancy word for therefore.

TOMOS   I thought there was a bit more to it than that.

LANA   Oh, that's enough about their psyches. Let's get
back to their bodies. After all we have to hold
the attention of the audience and we are now
competing with growling stomachs, the need for
food, for more booze, tired eyes, bulging bladders,
deadened nerve-endings in the buttocks.

— 136 —

TOMOS   They haven't been sitting *that* long. It's not bloody
        Wagner.

LANA    Okay, okay – allow me a little paranoia, can't you?

TOMOS   A little!

# ACT FOUR, SCENE SIX

LANA   The stage is awash with sheets. They are made of the finest cotton, the finest silk, satin, linen. They float and waft and shiver and drift sensuously, from above and from the wings, draped from wires, blown gently by fans, held aloft by immobile figures dressed in black.

TOMOS   What does it mean?

LANA   It is like watching the sea, up and down, up and down like – like waves.

TOMOS   Nice....but what are we meant to understand?

LANA   We are inside her mind. I am setting the scene here.

TOMOS   Ah.

LANA   The mind of the female, before it – oh, never mind about that now. The mind of the female, the mind of *this* female...

TOMOS   [*Tentative*] Might be a good moment for music.

LANA   Of course! Thank you.

TOMOS   De nada.

LANA   De-what?

TOMOS   Don't mention it – that's what it is in Spanish.

LANA   I didn't know you could speak Spanish!

TOMOS   I can't. *Please, Thank you,* and *My friend will pay,*

— 138 —

that's it. Please continue.

LANA       What is her favourite music? No, wrong question. What are her favourite sounds? One is silence, the complete lack of sound....but that won't work.

TOMOS    Sometimes complete silence is very effective.

LANA       Yes, but not here. When audience members are deprived of sound they fall back on their own thoughts.

TOMOS    Would that be such a bad thing?

LANA       I want a little more control.

TOMOS    [*Aside*] Now there's an understatement.

LANA       What did you say?

TOMOS    Nothing. So – sounds, then. But what?

LANA       Birdsong.

TOMOS    Oh. Cool.

LANA       The exquisite song of the blackbird, the beautiful notes of the nightingale, the nostalgic fluting call of the cuckoo, the wistful hoot of the owl.

TOMOS    All at once?

LANA       The sounds are so distant and delicate they are like a veil, a veil of birdsong.

TOMOS    Hey, that's – that's pretty nice. And, you know, that really will be music.

LANA       Yes. The most natural kind.

TOMOS  ...I wish you'd let me read some of your stuff.

LANA  My stuff?

TOMOS  Your poetry.

LANA  I will...

TOMOS  But when?

LANA  One day.

TOMOS  [*Sarcastic*] Well, don't rush into anything, will you.

LANA  The scene is set. Enid enters slowly. She is naked.
In her mind, desire is swelling, out of nowhere,
she has no need of a male presence to feel desire.
It simply – arises in her though she has noticed
that it can be generated by watching pornography
– the good old in-and-out. Regardless of the actual
aforegoing stimulant, she is sexually aroused.
She moves among the shifting fabric, stroking
it, kissing it, swathing it around her body. She
sighs. The sheets are released from their tethers,
there are hundreds of them, they settle around
her, they pile up as thick as a mattress, making a
huge soft nest, sensuous, warm, soft, supremely
comfortable. She sinks onto it, stretches
luxuriously.

TOMOS  Nice.

LANA  Enter a second being, a male. He tramples the
wafting veils, impatiently tears them aside – they
are merely obstructions to his gaining access to her
nakedness– and they settle limply on the floor,

— 140 —

losing their significance, destroying her mood, killing her desire. Without the faintest hint of tact or finesse, he joins her on the bed. They roll around. What is in her mind is unable to find expression on the material plane. Horizontal, in the presence of this male being, she is blank, unresponsive, for reasons earlier elucidated. He has to assume – he assumes – that her pleasure is equal to his though he is not prepared to take steps to ensure this (nor will he ever be)...

TOMOS   In other words, he can't be bothered to get her in the mood.

LANA   Exactly. He is eaten up with desire for her body so he assumes that she has an equal desire for his. This, however, is not the case. In fact his naked body leaves her cold and, since foreplay is conspicuous by its absence, she has to fall back on politeness.

TOMOS   Politeness?!

LANA   Indeed. It is her conditioning at work. It is a woman's obligation to supply a man with what he needs. This removes all pleasure from her and generates a conflict within.

TOMOS   I should say so!

LANA   Does she do what he wants or does she listen to the whispered urgings inside herself telling her to exert her own wants. The former impulse is the stronger and dictates her behaviour. The latter is too weak to compete but its existence causes pain.

— 141 —

The resulting conflict leaves her face completely blank. He will come to call this blank expression her *frightened rabbit* look.

TOMOS   He sounds like a real sweety.

LANA   He is used to getting his own way. Let's leave them there.

*END OF ACT FOUR, SCENE SIX*

LANA      Imagine her pain when she first hears herself
          described that way.

TOMOS    What way?

LANA      As a frightened rabbit.

TOMOS    I can't....but I'll take your word for it.

LANA      You can't?

TOMOS    Imagine it.

LANA      Why not?

TOMOS    I have to have things spelled out, okay?

LANA      But that's what it's like for me.

TOMOS    What is?

LANA      Certain things make me cry.

TOMOS    Certain things?

LANA      All kinds of things.

TOMOS    Like what?

LANA      Like....like looking at a photograph.

TOMOS    Looking at a photograph makes you cry?

LANA      Not just any photograph....one that reminds me of
          something.

TOMOS    You're peculiar, you know that?

LANA      You mean a photograph cannot make you cry?

— 143 —

TOMOS   Don't sound so surprised. Come on, it's time to get
        back to the job in hand. I want some more scenery,
        music.

LANA    We keep getting distracted. What's the next thing
        on the list?

TOMOS   Search me. I've completely lost track.

LANA    But that's your function! You were bragging about
        it not two minutes ago.

TOMOS   I was?

LANA    Oh forget it, never mind. I'll just let my thoughts
        drift, shall I?

TOMOS   It's no good fuming. I'm not perfect.

LANA    What a perfectly lovely word...

TOMOS   What – perfect?

LANA    Fuming....fuming....it's exquisite...

TOMOS   ...

LANA    All right, all right. There is so much they do not
        know about each other. We know more about
        them then they know about each other.

TOMOS   It must be fun to play God.

LANA    Is that what I'm doing? I thought I was describing
        the endless fallout from God's famous handiwork.

TOMOS   God's famous handiwork – good name for a group,
        that.

LANA     I'm bored. I've dried up.

TOMOS   Would you like something to drink?

LANA     I was speaking meta–

TOMOS   I *know* you were speaking metaphorically.

LANA     Got any ideas?

TOMOS   You said something about a wedding dress?

LANA     Oh no, no, it's much too soon for that.

TOMOS   Well, what about that train journey?

LANA     The train journey....all right.

TOMOS   Good.

# ACT FOUR, SCENE SEVEN

LANA      They are coming to the end of their long trek across the aforementioned continent.

TOMOS      Would it kill you to remind us which one it was?

LANA      Kill me? Of course not, don't be so dramatic, it's North America.

TOMOS      Me dramatic?! I like that!!

LANA      She is about to board a train that will carry her back to her starting point. She is returning *home*.

TOMOS      Why *home*? Not another quotation.

LANA      No....though it should be pointed out that she has never known what it is to have a home, so it might as well be a quote....a quote from someone else's life, someone who knows what it means to have a home. Anyway, there they both are, on the platform of a train station, saying a tearful goodbye. Let us for a moment study his inner thoughts.

TOMOS      It was really interesting finding out about his nightmares, by the way.

LANA      Good. Thank you. Where was I?....a tearful goodbye, yes. He is seriously sizing her up as a potential long-term mate. He knows he has discovered a small gem amid the dross of his life and that he must hang onto it. He has not a single doubt that it is his right and good fortune to have found her. So – let us rip her away from him.

— 146 —

TOMOS   That's your modus operandi, ain't it?

LANA    Ain't?

TOMOS   Yeah – to make something bad happen just when
        things are going well – and vickee verka.

LANA    Vickee verka! Have you completely forgotten how
        to speak English! I don't want to seem intolerant
        but–

TOMOS   –Then don't say what you're about to say. It's
        all very well to apologise for being intolerant but
        you're nevertheless about to make your *intolerant*
        point, aren't you?

LANA    ...

TOMOS   Please continue. Rip them apart – if you must. But
        wait a minute, what was it you said right at the
        beginning? The bit about taking her from behind?
        You said they'd have to wait until – act four wasn't
        it? Well, here we are.

LANA    Oh, that.

TOMOS   Wouldn't that make for good theatre? He takes
        her from behind and then you rip them apart.

LANA    Like dogs.

TOMOS   That's not what I meant. I didn't say that.

LANA    I know. I was just torturing myself, that's all.

TOMOS   So? What about it?

LANA    Will night never come?...

— 147 —

TOMOS    Don't tell me – another quote, right? I thought so.
         Just do it.

LANA     I'll describe it, but I don't want to show it.

TOMOS    No way!! This is theatre, you have to show it!

LANA     Don't tell me what I can and cannot do! And you
         yourself seem to be more than a little interested in
         having this scene performed.

TOMOS    [*Close to breaking point*] But you must, don't you
         see? Credit me with a little artistic vision. You
         waved that gun in the first act, now you have to fire
         the damn thing.

LANA     Delightful image....they will just have to wait a
         little longer. Any of that brandy left?

                *END OF ACT FOUR, SCENE SEVEN*

TOMOS  Better not drink too much of that stuff, you'll lose
       your focus.

LANA   Don't you understand, that's exactly what I want?

TOMOS  That doesn't make sense.

LANA   Sense! I am sick and tired of making sense.

TOMOS  Then you shouldn't have got yourself into thi–

LANA   I'm going.

TOMOS  Going?! Going where?

LANA   I don't know, I'm off, that's all. Where's my
       coat...

TOMOS  But you – you can't! What about the
       performance?! The audience!

LANA   They can rot, for all I care! They can stick a finger
       up their own arses.

TOMOS  What's the matter? Why are you being like this?
       What's got into you?

LANA   [*Acid*] And which of those questions shall I respond
       to first.

TOMOS  Don't do this, I beg you.

LANA   Beg me! Whose side are you on really? Because you
       don't seem to be on mine.

TOMOS  There are no sides, there's only art. Artistic
       endeavour. You owe it to us.

LANA   Owe it to you?!?! BALDERDASH!!! [*Violent exit*]

\* \* \*

VOICE   [*Distant*] Ladies and gentlemen, we apologise for the delay, but we are having a slight technical problem. Please remain seated while we fix it. This should take only a minute or two. Again, our apologies and thank you for your patience.

\* \* \*

LANA    All right, iss time.

TOMOS   Where the hell have you been!! The audience is creating merry hell – half of them have already walked out.

LANA    I don't give a ffflying fffuckhh.

TOMOS   You're drunk!

LANA    Iss the only way I'm gonna get through thiss.

TOMOS   Let me make you some coffee.

LANA    'kay... No, on second thoughts, I juss wanna get thiss over with.

TOMOS   Go ahead. I can hear the determination in your voice.

LANA    Yeah, thass me, determined. Ha!

TOMOS   Go on, go ahead.

LANA    ...I wanna say something about nipples...

TOMOS   Be my guest.

LANA    No, I mean, back there. I almost fell into a – a –

— 150 —

trap.

TOMOS   What trap?

LANA   Describing it – from a man's point of view.

TOMOS   What are you *talking* about? We need to get on here.

LANA   Female – um – thingumeejig – you know – female whatchamacallit. I described it from a man's point of view.

TOMOS   I don't remember. Are you sure you wouldn't like some black coffee?

LANA   So it was memorable, huh?....no, no coffee.

TOMOS   Okay, go ahead. As quickly as you can.

LANA   Right. I'm sobering up now. I once heard a man say, *I know how to stiffen a nipple.* Men think iss the first sign of sexual alou – aroul – arousal.

TOMOS   So? Isn't it? Is this part of the scene now?

LANA   Iss not true! When a nipple's touched it constracss – it contracss. Iss involuntary. Iss not necessella – not necessarily a sign of ar-al-arousal.

TOMOS   [*Brisk*] I see. I didn't know that.

LANA   Just wanna explode that myth.

TOMOS   [*Brisker*] Okay – thanks. I'll try and remember that.

LANA   You can stiffen a nipple with a dead *rattt.*

— 151 —

TOMOS  [*Briskest*] Charming – the *scene*?

LANA  Okay, here goes. I'm a bit more with it now. Perhaps I will have that coffee.

## ACT FOUR, SCENE EIGHT

LANA    [*A deep breath*] He has her stand on a box with her back to him.

TOMOS    What's the setting? What's the time of day? Where are they?!

LANA    A bedroom – middle-of-the-road décor and furniture. broad daylight. She is standing on a small wooden box, he is behind her, inches away, filled with admiration of this body that he thinks he owns. Her legs are slightly apart, she is bent over their bed with her palms flat on the quilt – her body is at a right angle where the legs meet the torso....so that their genitals are on the same horizontal plane. She is bracing herself, mentally and physically for the – the unwanted... He is already salivating at the prospect of the effortless – oh god – I'm so tired of that damned word.

TOMOS    Which word?

LANA    You know which word!

TOMOS    Use some other word then – make something up!

LANA    Forget it. She bends over and presents her arse to him. He forges into her, she is not wet.... she is merely doing her duty....so he spits on his palm, out of consideration....to himself. She steels herself for the encounter, wills the muscles in her vagina to relax, prepares to take it. He cannot see her face, fortunately....so she can wince openly. The sight of the engorged, pinkish-purple, spit-lubricated tube disappearing into the hole and emerging again is almost enough to make him swoon. He is worshipping at the altar of sex. He is communing with his god. One of his gods.... and what are they, these gods of his?....money, sugar, sex, not necessarily in that order. His left hand is on her left haunch, the right hand on her right so that he can exquisitely control the rhythm of his pumping. She bends further forward, rests her forehead on her palms, moaning convincingly so that it will be over faster, though despairing inwardly, and watches her slackened stomach lurch in time to the onslaught. There is a moment when she knows he will not be able to turn back – she could write a post-graduate thesis about that moment....and the reinforcement of her conviction that any arse would do, so long as the hole is tight enough. Her hole is good and tight....never having been stretched to breaking by a fully developed foetus propelling itself into the world. A mixed blessing. He comes to the peak of his excitement – only one thing left: the squirt of cloudy viscous fluid into her body. She can relax properly now, it's over.

TOMOS   My god, that's strong stuff, but they'll love it. Where are you going–

LANA   –I think I'm going to be sick.

*END OF ACT FOUR, SCENE EIGHT*

TOMOS   There you are. I didn't know whether to come after
        you or not.

LANA    I'm all right now.

TOMOS   You're white as a sheet. Are you sure you're okay?

LANA    I'm fine. I am where I need to be to continue.

TOMOS   Glad to hear it.

LANA    Music. That's what's needed.

TOMOS   Was there music during that last scene?

LANA    No. Complete silence.

TOMOS   Are you sure about that? I'd have thought
        something a bit – off, you know – would work.

LANA    Off?

TOMOS   Yeah, I mean–

LANA    You're right, you're right. [*Breaks down*] You're
        right! Oh!

TOMOS   What's wrong? What's the matter?

LANA    I don't know how to – to – oh, can you ever
        forgive me for my endless *sturm und drang*? All I do
        is make both of us suffer.

TOMOS   I'm not suffering. What's shtormentrang?

LANA    You're not?

TOMOS   No! My life would be pretty empty without –
        without all these jobs I'm doing.

— 155 —

LANA      Jobs? What jobs?

TOMOS   I mean *this* job.

LANA      That's how you think of it? As a job?

TOMOS   I mean this work, that's what I should have said.
          I'm enjoying all the different aspects of this work,
          keeps me on my toes. It's interesting, all the push
          and pull, you know? I know I'm alive. I've never
          done anything like this before. Usually it's the
          complete opposite, total boredom.

LANA      Really?

TOMOS   Really. Now, moving right along, you mentioned
          music.

LANA      But I was led to believe you volunteered for this...

TOMOS   I did. But I had a choice, and I chose you.

LANA      You *chose* me?

TOMOS   Yeah. They warned me you'd be the most difficult
          to handle so I thought – why not? I like a challenge
          – no, that's not it – I *need* a challenge, that's it.

LANA      Why have we not talked about this before?

TOMOS   You never asked.

LANA      [*Chastised*] That's true. What were the other
          choices?

TOMOS   You mean who were they? A composer, a painter,
          a sculptor, an architect. I'm not allowed to tell you
          their names.

— 156 —

LANA    I promise I won't breathe a word. *Who are they?*

TOMOS   'Fraid not. Can't do it.

LANA    I'll get it out of you.

TOMOS   No, you won't. I don't break my word.

LANA    I see, I see. Well, let's get back to the job in hand, shall we?

TOMOS   And I had actually read some of your stuff.

LANA    Which piece?

TOMOS   It was a short story, I can't recall the title – something about tea, was it?

LANA    *The Importance of Tea!* You read that?

TOMOS   Mm-hmm.

LANA    And what was it that you liked about it?

TOMOS   I didn't say I liked it. Look, we'll talk about it later.

LANA    Later? You throw out a criticism like that and then say we'll talk about it later!

TOMOS   You're doing it again! We need to get back to *now*.

LANA    Grrr. You can be quite irritating yourself, you know. You *promise* we'll talk about it later?

TOMOS   I promise.

LANA    I'll hold you to it.

TOMOS   I know you will. Now – music. I think that last

scene – the one that made you throw up – needs music. I'm sure of it.

LANA   You're right. You've inspired me!

# ACT FOUR, SCENE NINE

LANA      The music is dissonant....jarring, lacking in melody, unharmonious, umm, disagreeable. The instruments of the orchestra seem to be fighting amongst themselves. No sooner have the violins played a jagged dissonant phrase than the trombones blare their disagreement, the cellos charge into the fray, arcing violently between highest and lowest register, then the trumpets start bleating in strident argument – the woodwi–

TOMOS      [*Flat*] No.

LANA      No? Why not? What do you suggest then?

TOMOS      That would be overkill. Like the music in a Hitchcock film – it tells the audience what to think.

LANA      [*Feigned stab to the chest*] Aargh, we can't have that. What do you suggest?

TOMOS      Something extremely romantic. Lush, sentimental.

LANA      Never!

TOMOS      You like incongruity, right? This is one place where it will really work.

LANA      My god, you're right. You're right, you're right. Why didn't I think of that!

TOMOS      Sometimes you're too close to your material.

LANA      Ouch!

TOMOS   Any suggestions?

LANA    Well, there's Rachmaninov....or Tchaikovsky....
        Mahler perhaps.

TOMOS   Streisand.

LANA    What!

TOMOS   Barbra Streisand – that thing she sings about
        people needing people.

LANA    [*Aghast*] *A feeling deep in your soul, says you were half
        now you're whole. People who need people...*

TOMOS   One of the worst songs you ever heard in your life.

LANA    I think I may throw up again. It's perfect.

TOMOS   Told ya.

*END OF ACT FOUR, SCENE NINE*

LANA    I just had a thought....tell me if you think it works...

TOMOS   Happy to.

LANA    Those Royal weddings – did you ever see one?

TOMOS   Not really interested in that stuff.

LANA    Well, any wedding then – a white one, I mean
        – with all the – the trimmings or whatever the
        word is for all that nonsense, not to mention the
        ludicrous expense, the organ, the congregation,
        the hats – oh, don't forget the hats! And those
        vows! – *till death do us part* – *to have and to hold* and
        all that guff.

TOMOS   What are you getting at? What's your point?

LANA    *Those whom God has joined together let no-one put
        asunder.* Don't you just love that *whhhoomm.* Mm?
        Oh, you know me – my love of extremes. Let's
        juxtapose the good and the bad, the positive and
        negative aspects of being married.

TOMOS   Okay, I'm with you now.

LANA    How extreme should I make it?

TOMOS   As extreme as you like!

LANA    A scenic journey through the – the ups and downs
        of married life. On the one hand joy, on the other,
        sorrow. Or whatever words you want to use.

TOMOS   I hope you won't mind me suggesting it – again
        – but this sounds like an ideal moment for
        projections.

— 161 —

LANA      Good idea. The positive aspects projected – in the
          round perhaps, all over the walls of the auditorium
          – everywhere, even though, in some places, like –
          like the curtains, the ceiling, they may not be very
          clear. And the negative aspects enacted fully lit –
          clear as day – on the stage.

TOMOS     No – the other way around.

LANA      The other way around?

TOMOS     Use the stage for the good bits.

LANA      You think?

TOMOS     Yeah. Have the positive aspects – the picnic of
          married life – be the action on stage, well lit, clear.

LANA      O-k-a-y...

TOMOS     So then the projections around the auditorium are
          distorted – I mean obscured – by what they are
          being projected against. That will make what's
          happening in *them* – the sexual fiasco of married
          life – not so clear but more intriguing because it's
          X-rated. It'll give a sense of being a voyeur.

LANA      Brilliant!!! The picnic and the fiasco. Let's do it!

TOMOS     Glad you like it.

LANA      But I'll have to say no to the Streisand.

TOMOS     You said you liked it!

LANA      Too cheap.

TOMOS     Well, what music *are* you going to use then?

— 162 —

ACT FIVE

## ACT FIVE, SCENE ONE

LANA    The 1812.

TOMOS   What?

LANA    Tchaikovsky's 1812 overture.

TOMOS   The one with the cannons?

LANA    It will be amazingly distracting – disturbing – you
        know? And what with the other stuff going on,
        the action on stage, the images on the walls of the
        auditorium, they won't know if they are coming or
        going!

TOMOS   Meaning the audience?

LANA    Yes!

*END OF ACT FIVE, SCENE ONE*

TOMOS   Hmmm...

LANA    What? You don't think it works?

TOMOS   Mmm....d'you mind – do you mind if I say
        something a little off the subject? It's something
        you probably won't like.

LANA    Shoot.

TOMOS   Shoot? Where did that come from!

LANA    [*Harsh*] The ionosphere.

TOMOS   Don't get defensive.

LANA    Just say it.

TOMOS   You don't....no... I want to be very precise–

LANA    –That would make a change.

TOMOS   [*Calm*] Stop it. I just want to make an observation –
        about you.

LANA    You're going to say I hate men.

TOMOS   No, because I don't think you do.

LANA    [*Nervous*] Go on then.

TOMOS   In my opinion, you're afraid of being loved. Only
        my opinion.

## ACT FIVE, SCENE TWO

LANA [*Hurried delivery*] Okay, so – uh – moving right along – here we are at the – uh – the – um – at scene two of – of – uh – whichever act it is now – five, I think. Our – um – our antagonists – no, I won't use that any longer – you were right, I was just trying to be original – silly! – where was I? – our *pro*tagonists have been revealed in all their glory – and lack of it! Ha! And [*bluster*] I *think* I've made my *point* about the *mess* that passes for married *life* and – and– so now, we see them–we see them–yes, um, we see them–they–we–they–we– [*gasps for air*]

TOMOS It was time to say it. I've been wanting to ever since...

LANA [*Confused*] We – we – we see them slumped – correction! – he is slumped – being satisfied and spent – across the matrimonial bed – after that sweet little example of – of – why matrimonial? – when that's where most of the patrimonial action takes place – where was I? – while she lies next to him, numb, bruised....um....uh....used. She – she –

TOMOS ...Ever since I read that story of yours.

LANA She is used to feeling this way – correction! – no! – she will never get used to feeling this way, it's like – it's – it's like – god, how sloppy I'm getting – I mean, it's *as if* – it's as if – where was I? – it's – um – it's as if there is a – you said you didn't like that story!

— 165 —

TOMOS    No, I didn't say that.

LANA     Oh but you did. That's exactly what you said – *I didn't say I liked it.*

TOMOS    No – I loved it.

LANA     You....loved...

TOMOS    What I mean is that I felt a really strong empathy for the woman – the person – who wrote it.

LANA     Meaning me.

TOMOS    Obviously. Why don't you go on with the scene?

LANA     [*Thrown*] Go on with the scene? Go on with the – [*dazed*]

TOMOS    We can talk about this other stuff later, I promise.

LANA     Later....yes, all right. Yes, I'll go on with the scene. A change of scene, perhaps....where was I? She lies beside him, feeling the way she always does at these times....numb, bruised, used....you really loved it? Honestly?

TOMOS    It moved me. I felt I understood her – well, a little – the author.

LANA     Meaning me again.

TOMOS    I wanted to try and find out a bit more about her. And the best way to do that was to read everything she had written.

LANA     What about the audience? They're probably getting restless again.

— 166 —

TOMOS   They're your responsibility.

LANA    I'll go on with the next scene then, shall I....you read everything?

TOMOS   I gave it my best shot.

LANA    I didn't think men functioned like that.

TOMOS   This one does.

*Pause*

LANA    ...How old are you?

TOMOS   About ten years older than I look.

LANA    So....we're about the same age...

TOMOS   Yes. [*Gently*] Go on with the scene.

LANA    The scene....uh – yes....well, um, the worst part of this situation for her is that she has now begun to feel – to feel....I can't.

TOMOS   But the worst is over.

LANA    What on earth do you mean by that?

TOMOS   Is there anything left to describe that's worse than what you've just described?

LANA    Yes – no – yes – I don't know. You're wrong, you know!

TOMOS   About what?

LANA    I'm not afraid – of being loved. That's not it.

TOMOS    I know. I didn't express myself clearly. I should
         have said you have never allowed anyone to really
         love you.

LANA     That's not true either. Oh hell, it is, it is true! I've
         done it, haven't I?

TOMOS    Done what?

LANA     The very thing you told me not to. I've confused
         authenticity with catharsis.

TOMOS    But don't you get it? For you they are the same
         thing. That's where the magic lies.

LANA     Magic....do I believe in magic?

TOMOS    Definitely.

LANA     Magic.

TOMOS    Finish the scene.

LANA     All right. I'll go on with the scene now. The
         worst part of this situation for her is that she has
         now begun to feel vaguely aroused. Not being
         completely immune to stimulation she has begun
         to feel a hint of desire though she has her own
         ideas of how lovemaking should proceed. So she
         lies there, tortured by her own feelings, wanting
         to be wanted the way *she* wants to be wanted,
         taken the way *she* wants to be taken. She feels
         herself slowly dying from the need to – [*whispered*]
         surrender...

TOMOS    What was that last bit?

— 168 —

LANA     Oh nothing. We'll just leave her lying there, thinking her thoughts.

*END OF ACT FIVE, SCENE TWO*

LANA    You know....I waved two other – um – thingies
        around back there.

TOMOS   Thingies?

LANA    Y'know – *You waved it around in the first act, now
        you have to fire the damn thing.*

TOMOS   A gun?

LANA    I don't much like that word.

TOMOS   It's just a word. So what were they, these other
        things?

LANA    I hope you understand that I am practically
        exploding with curiosity about you.

TOMOS   I promise to answer *all* your questions once you've
        finished this – this current project. I'm looking
        forward to it.

LANA    [*Encouraged*] All right. Next scene, whatever it is.
        The train journey.

TOMOS   The train journey! I'd almost forgotten about it!

LANA    And where are we now?

TOMOS   Act five, scene three.

## ACT FIVE, SCENE THREE

LANA     Enid carries with her onto the train the image of
         Marvin's tear-stained face and an unbuttoned
         white shirt cuff–

TOMOS    –the white cuff! At last!

LANA     – plus her one piece of luggage and a clutch of
         photographs, taken during her long journey. The
         stage darkens, we hear her sobbing. No! I've got
         it! Scrub all that. Oh, you'll love this, I can't resist.
         Let's go back to the end of the scene that sickened
         me. They are lying side by side in the marriage bed,
         him spent, her numb. The lights go down on the
         recumbent couple. Are you with me? Suddenly,
         without any kind of warning, there is complete
         silence – which will be shocking after the racket of
         the 1812.

TOMOS    I'm still voting for Streisand.

LANA     So – music – loud music and then – suddenly –
         complete darkness and complete silence, so the
         audience falls silent, out of concern that some
         new technical hitch has occurred. The hiatus I
         engineered earlier has rattled them – *What else can
         happen?*, they think. The silence is full of tension.
         Then we hear his voice, it says: *Again*. And we
         know what that means. Oh, thank christ, I've
         found a way to continue. His voice says, softly but
         firmly, *Again* and we know what that means. There
         are groans and creaks and bumps as the bodies on
         the bed begin to move, it's starting up again–

— 171 —

TOMOS  Wait!

LANA  Yes?

TOMOS  I'm not sure if this is the best moment to say it, but
I have to tell you it's been really difficult for me
to listen to you put yourself through all this pain.
Very difficult.

LANA  The worst is over. You said so yourself.

TOMOS  No more descriptions of bad sex?

LANA  No.

TOMOS  Not that I want to influence your artistic choices,
but....you did use the word engineered.

LANA  Did I? Don't worry about me, I'm fine, I'm
rolling again, that's all I care about. Let me set
the scene here. I tried to do it a while back, do
you recall? The creaks and squeaks and bumps
become more regular, louder, and the orchestra
supplies a droning accompaniment which serves
as a counterpoint to sounds from the bed and also
reassures the audience that this is planned. The
creaking and squeaking and bumping speeds up –
our imagination does the rest. These unequivocal
sounds gradually morph into the equally
unequivocal, readily recognisable sounds of a train
moving swiftly along a track. Diddly-dum, diddly-
dee, diddly-dum, diddly-dee.

TOMOS  Don't forget what I said about adverbs.

LANA  Noted. The lights come up, the bed is gone, we

— 172 —

are now in a train station and there they are, Enid
and Marvin, hugging each other at the end of
a busy train station platform. They have moved
away from the crowd, they have managed to find a
place where they can wait, relatively undisturbed,
for the train she is about to catch. She is going
home, remember? – correction – she is going back
to place where she currently lives. Bright light,
bustle, luggage, foreign accents – foreign to her,
that is, he is on home turf. They are both weeping.
Departures always get the waterworks going for
her and he – he can hardly bear the thought that
he has discovered a small gem amid the dross of
his life and is about to lose it. The train arrives,
she boards. She carries with her onto the train the
image of his tear-stained face and an unbuttoned
white shirt cuff.

TOMOS   I thought they'd already parted.

LANA   I've jumped into the past, to the first parting,
when I had to rip her away from him, remember?

TOMOS   Okay.

LANA   Shall she continue to cry? Oh dear me, yes. After
the train has pulled out of the station and she has
taken her seat, she looks through her photographs
and cries so hard that a man sitting across the aisle
from her becomes very concerned but does not
dare offer assistance. The train rocks from side to
side as if trying to quell this outpouring. Why is
she crying so much?

TOMOS   I was about to ask that.

— 173 —

LANA     Think back.

TOMOS    They won't want to.

LANA     Who?

TOMOS    The audience.

LANA     You're right. Audiences do not want to think. Then
         I shall think back for them, to an earlier iteration
         of the same question, to which the answer was: her
         fragile heart.

TOMOS    I think you said her tender heart.

LANA     I did? Okay. Same difference. Her heart is both
         tender and fragile. This is a woman whose heart is
         made of – of pulled sugar.

TOMOS    What?!

LANA     No, that won't do.

TOMOS    Why not?

LANA     Your reaction said it all!

TOMOS    Sometimes I'm shocked by your daring. It doesn't
         mean it's not good.

LANA     [Wary] Go on.

TOMOS    It was a bit of a shock, that's all, because I never
         heard it before – but that's – you know – okay.

LANA     Hearing an expression one has not heard before is
         always slightly shocking though not necessarily in
         a negative way.

— 174 —

TOMOS   That's what I said, didn't I?

LANA    Hmmm....I do like flinging open closed doors...

TOMOS   You like flinging, period.

LANA    Period?

TOMOS   Sorry, full stop. Go on. Go on talking about her pulled sugar heart.

LANA    It sounds stupid put that way.

TOMOS   It's not stupid!

LANA    Well, I no longer like it. It does not fit. I shall find another – expression.

TOMOS   Now you're being difficult.

LANA    I merely strive for – for – perfection.

TOMOS   Yeah, and perfectionists are a pain in the neck.

LANA    I'm not sure I should be putting up with this. You are becoming more bold than is acceptable in this situation.

TOMOS   Stop talking like a textbook and get on with the story. I have limits too, you know.

LANA    What happened to all that empathy and admiration?

TOMOS   Just tell us what's in the photographs.

LANA    He and she; him; her; him and her; her and him; them; the two of them; the occasional appearance of other beings; some interesting settings. She will,

— 175 —

at a later date, on the other side of the Atlantic, show this collection of photos to another, who will smile and say to her, *You know, there's only one star in this show.* What this person means is the ubiquitous presence of Marvin.

TOMOS   Who are you talking about?

LANA   ...

TOMOS   Oh, ex*cuse* me. About whom are you talking?

LANA   I've jumped into the future now. It doesn't matter, it's just someone whose opinion she treasures and whose approval she craves. A more perceptive individual, someone who is less biased towards her efforts and knows how to read between the lines of the images, would note that the real star of the show is Enid. Whenever she appears in a photograph she shines, she glows, she – what's another word like that?

TOMOS   Uh...

LANA   No matter. She thinks she is not photogenic but photographs of her reveal a clarity that is muddied in real life by her – by her...

TOMOS   I'm bored. Sorry, but I am. Get back to the train. Throw something into the black hole. Pull some more sugar. What's so special about that damned shirt cuff anyway?

LANA   She has never before encountered a man who routinely leaves his shirt cuffs open and hanging. For her, it is the equivalent – subconsciously – of

— 176 —

the elaborate lace spilling from the sleeve of an eighteenth century fop, an affectation. The reason it sticks in her mind is because, during their tearful parting, her head was lowered so its image was fixed there.

TOMOS  Fair enough.

*END OF ACT FIVE, SCENE THREE*

TOMOS   So what's this about pulled sugar?

LANA    Have you ever heard of the MOF?

TOMOS   Muff?

LANA    No – MOF, M-O-F. It stands for Meilleurs Ouvriers de France.

TOMOS   Does it now?

LANA    Don't mock.

TOMOS   You'll have to transl–

LANA    *Translation*: The finest workmen of France. It's an organization that holds a contest every – every year, I think – to find the best artisans in France, in various fields of endeavour. The one I am referring to is the pastry chef category – oh, does anyone care about this?

TOMOS   Is it relevant?

LANA    You're the one who asked for details. All right, I've started so I suppose I'd better finish. Each contestant, an accomplished chef in his own right – and they *are* still mostly men–

TOMOS   –Okay, *okay*.

LANA    Each chef has to create and construct a culinary work of art almost entirely out of sugar: colourful, elaborate, aesthetically pleasing, consumable though not, in this instance, intended for consumption but to impress the judges.

TOMOS   Why? What's the point?

— 178 —

LANA     To demonstrate skill. The main challenge is in the preparation and handling of the chief ingredient. As you no doubt know, sugar, when warmed to a high temperature, becomes a liquid mass and, after slight cooling, can be pulled and twisted and twirled and folded into a huge variety of shapes.

TOMOS   You know very well I didn't know that.

LANA     Well now you do. It must be kept warm to allow for further manipulation because it cools rapidly and once set, is incredibly brittle. The slightest movement can cause breakage. This pulled sugar is used in concoctions that sometimes look like a swirl of pretty ribbons – at first glance they look as if they are made out of glass rising from the surfaces of the pastry boards on which they are constructed. The creation that displays the highest degree of skill, has the most aesthetic appeal and can survive the journey from the chef's work area to the judges' table wins. The winner gets a special collar – red, white and blue, of course.

TOMOS   So....the analogy – is that the right word? – with Enid is: very pleasing but very breakable. Is that right?

LANA     No, not Enid herself, but her heart. Okay, I've got it – the whole thing! Next scene.

## ACT FIVE, SCENE FOUR

LANA    Through the wonderful magic and trickery of modern theatre, we will split the stage into two levels, upper and lower. On the upper level Enid sits in a train carriage, looking through her photographs and sobbing uncontrollably. On the lower level a number of chefs walk on, each carrying, on a large pastry board, with the utmost care, a structure made entirely of pulled sugar – or glass, the effect will be the same. This is wholly appropriate as, to Marvin, Enid represents sweetness, the metaphysical sweetness he feels he has been so denied, whereas in reality he consumes a great deal of the actual stuff. One look at his teeth will confirm this....you're very quiet.

TOMOS    I'm not sure I can take much more of this. Why do you keep torturing yourself?

LANA    I don't know. Just go then. You're free to leave.

TOMOS    Just like that?

LANA    Yes.

TOMOS    What about my contract?

LANA    I release you from it.

TOMOS    But you'll still pay me the full whack?

LANA    Half.

TOMOS    Half!

LANA    Five eighths.

TOMOS    ...What the hell, I'll stay.

LANA     Make your mind up.

TOMOS    That's a very odd expression, don't you think?

LANA     Odd. Yes.

TOMOS    My mind is made up – that's absurd. What was it
         before it was *made up*?

LANA     You're right – I'm not sure I can take much more
         of this either.

TOMOS    Forget it. I'm not going anywhere. I'll fulfill my
         contract, I'll try to have a better attitude. I'll stay.

LANA     Good, I'm glad.

TOMOS    Well, that helps....because I care about you.

LANA     You– Where was I?

TOMOS    Two levels.

LANA     Y-e-s....two levels. Each chef – each contestant –
         who enters on the lower level of the stage carries,
         arms carefully extended, a colourful towering
         sugar/glass edifice, horizontal on a large piece of
         board. This is his oeuvre, his *tour de force*. There is
         a large table downstage right, to the right of which
         stand several judges with unsmiling faces – they
         are ready to be extremely critical. They are known
         for the severity of their judgements. This is where
         each chef is headed. The instant the first contestant
         places his oeuvre on this table, it collapses.

TOMOS    The table?

— 181 —

LANA  The oeuvre. Being extraordinarily fragile, the edifice collapses into a useless heap of shattered sugar shards.

TOMOS  I like that.

LANA  You're a fan of alliteration.

TOMOS  Am I?

LANA  It's all right, most people are. After each collapse a young woman in a maid's uniform rushes on with a broom and large metal dustpan to dispose of the fragments. They are swept into the dustpan with a satisfying smash and crash and clatter.

TOMOS  And the orchestra?

LANA  What do you mean *and the orchestra*?

TOMOS  For the noise.

LANA  Oh. Good idea. Cymbals perhaps.

TOMOS  At least.

LANA  On the upper level, Enid continues to shuffle through her photos and cry. We'll use the viola section for that – sobbing sounds. She was a contralto in the school choir so that's appropriate. From time to time the concerned man across the aisle starts to rise from his seat, with the intention of going over to comfort her, but each time, thinks the better of it, sits down again, looks out of the window, brow furrowed. He has never felt so torn.

TOMOS  I know how he feels.

LANA    I feel like doing something ridiculous.

TOMOS   Then do it.

LANA    On the lower level of the stage, the dozen or so
        chefs have experienced their culinary trauma and
        departed. They now return to the stage en masse,
        remove their chef's white neckerchiefs and wave
        to the train. End of scene. You're laughing, that's
        good.

TOMOS   I was thinking a bit beyond that – no, you won't
        like it.

LANA    Try me.

TOMOS   You'll hate it.

LANA    Tell me!

TOMOS   Okay. I just thought it would be – since they
        are French, right? Wouldn't it be funny – no, I
        can't – okay, okay – I thought it would be really
        hilarious to have them stand in a line waving their
        neckerchiefs and doing – no, I can't say it, you'll
        be so insulted – okay, okay! – stand in a line doing
        the – the Can-Can!

LANA    [*Flat*] The Can-Can.

TOMOS   I'm sorry!! I'll leave now.

LANA    But – that's brilliant!

TOMOS   It is?

LANA    I absolutely *love* it.

— 183 —

TOMOS   You do?

LANA    It will be so – so infuriating – to the romantics in
        the audience, the ones who have felt her pain and
        have been very moved by her sobbing.

TOMOS   Totally!

LANA    We'll shovel it all into the black hole – chefs,
        sugar, dust pan and brush, neckerchiefs, train
        passengers, her copious tears, everything. End of
        scene.

        *END OF ACT FIVE, SCENE FOUR*

LANA    Your – dissatisfaction obviously served a purpose.

TOMOS   Did it?

LANA    Isn't that where the idea came from?

TOMOS   Maybe. So where is she going now? She has to cross the Atlantic and she can't do that by train.

LANA    Washington D.C., from where she started out.

<u>ACT SIX</u>

# ACT SIX, SCENE ONE

LANA     Washington D.C. This is where she began her journey. There is a couple there, a married couple, John and Julie, whom she has known for many years. They treat her a little like a child, even though she is several years older than either of them. They want a child of their own....perhaps without realising it, they are practising on her. She allows this because she is aware of their deep desire to become parents and because she is very fond of them. John and Julie....there is a sweetness between them which does not repel her. They were very concerned that she intended to travel across the country alone. But....how to convey this state of affairs?

TOMOS     What state of affairs?

LANA     Her being patronised by her nice friends – oh, hell, I'm stuck again.

TOMOS     You need a dead body.

LANA     A *what*?!

TOMOS     Can't fail. In a murder mystery, when the action looks like it's flagging, throw in another corpse. In a romance –

LANA     It's not a romance!

TOMOS     Sorry – tragedy. Even better. In a tragedy, when the action looks like it's flagging, throw in the equivalent of a dead body.

LANA       Which is?

TOMOS   More sex.

LANA       Ah.

TOMOS   Married sex – the good kind.

LANA       Is there such a thing?

TOMOS   Of course there is.

LANA       I'm too cynical, that's my trouble.

TOMOS   I know.

LANA       More sex, you said? All right. [*Slowly*] Enid knows
           that John and Julie make love at the optimum
           time for conception – Julie has told her this. A
           thermometer and a small calendar are beside
           the sink in the bathroom and Julie takes her
           temperature every day. When she is ready –
           not for sex per se but for sex that might lead to
           pregnancy – she drops her hint – gently – to John
           who is reading the sports page in a newspaper. He,
           being a man, is ready at a moment's notice. He
           too wants a child but for now all he cares about is
           the prospect of pleasure – the pleasure of making
           himself one with her, knowing he has the ability to
           deliver the necessary seed. He has proved himself
           in the fertility clinic with a plastic cup and a copy
           of Penthouse. He loves Julie and wants to make her
           pregnant, she adores him and wants to give him a
           child. What could be more natural?

TOMOS   Is that a rhetorical question?

— 187 —

LANA     Let us follow them into the bedroom, let us watch
         them disrobe. Let us observe their initial kisses and
         caresses, their....accouplement. Yes, that ought to
         do it.

TOMOS    Good, that's good. Straightforward consensual sex.

LANA     A pleasant domestic scene – unlike anything we
         have encountered up till now. Missionary position.

TOMOS    The audience will find that comforting.

LANA     Afterwards Julie lies on her back, arms hugging
         her bent legs against her chest. Her doctor has told
         her this helps with conception. John goes back to
         reading his newspaper.

TOMOS    Too cynical. He cares about her, you said so
         yourself.

LANA     What then?

TOMOS    He makes her a cup of tea – her favourite,
         whatever that is.

LANA     Ooooo-long.

TOMOS    Sounds good.

LANA     I made it up. I thought it sounded better than
         Lipton's.

TOMOS    Doesn't matter. It has a ring to it.

LANA     The lights go down on this touching scene.

*END OF ACT SIX, SCENE ONE*

— 188 —

LANA    You were very helpful with that scene...

TOMOS  My pleasure.

LANA    Are you – married, yourself?

TOMOS  I was.

LANA    Divorced?

TOMOS  Widower.

LANA    But you're too young to be a widower.

TOMOS  It's taken me a couple of years to stop thinking
       that.

LANA    May I ask what happened – d'you mind talking
       about it?

TOMOS  Not now.

LANA    Why not?

TOMOS  We have to get on here.

LANA    Look, if this relation – if this – arrangement is
       going to work you have to be completely open and
       honest with me.

TOMOS  Don't forget the audience.

LANA    Oh, bugger them.

TOMOS  But they want to know what happens next.

LANA    So do I!

TOMOS  Okay, okay. Finish this act and I'll tell you. I want

— 189 —

to tell you, believe me. But let's get to the end of this act first.

LANA     *God*, you're a hard taskmaster.

# ACT SIX, SCENE TWO

LANA  Enid skates around the edge of the black hole, as if on a razor's edge, creating a black line in the diffused light.

TOMOS  Literally?

LANA  Sure. Why not? In her sweet, short-skirted skating outfit edged with fur that shows off her legs. The fur is not real. There is a note in the programme to that effect.

TOMOS  Is that necessary?

LANA  One has to be politically correct these days.

TOMOS  No, one doesn't. We are all sick of that. Leave it out.

LANA  Okay, the fur is real. Enid has never wanted to marry, has never wanted a child. The audience, however, has not been made aware of this. Enid expected her journey to remain solitary – she expected to remain a lone traveller. It was what she wanted. She thinks she functions best alone. But the audience does not know this. Wants the opposite in fact. She is a woman alone, therefore she must have a male companion, a man must appear. The line she skates along spreads out, she is now skating on a frozen lake. The entire stage is a frozen lake, the scenery frosted. Other skaters arrive, in couples, some with small children whom they tow carefully along on the treacherous icy surface. She is the only one skating alone. She

— 191 —

continues to skate, quite skilfully, but then she slips, falls, lands on the cold hard ice, lies immobile for a few moments. Out of nowhere a lone skater – a man – suddenly appears and helps her up. They smile at each other. He releases her and she brushes crumbs of ice off her outfit, fluffs up her fur. He offers her his hand, she takes it, they skate slowly to the edge of the lake and disappear.

TOMOS    Touch of Swan Lake there?

LANA    If you like. When faced with the possibility of becoming part of a couple she did not resist. The only person surprised by this development was Enid. The audience were not surprised – they were anticipating it, hoping for it, *expecting* it. But before we know it, she returns to the ice and continues to skate among the couples with their tottering offspring. Alone. The audience sighs a collective sigh: *It didn't work out.* The disappointment is palpable. [*Pause*] Why have I destroyed so many of their illusions?

TOMOS    It's because *your* illusions have been shattered. Wasn't that your intention? To make them feel that?

LANA    Yes.

TOMOS    You haven't shattered any illusions – you've just made people aware they have them.

LANA    Isn't that the same thing?

*END OF ACT SIX, SCENE TWO*

LANA    Well, now I've managed to make myself utterly miserable.

TOMOS   Don't despair, you'll get going again.

LANA    That's easy for you to say. All right, I have it. For this we need the revolving stage – the one we used for the teetering dancers in act – whatever it was...

TOMOS   ...Two.

LANA    You actually remember?

TOMOS   I've been taking notes.

LANA    Of course. Her encounters with men – especially in the bedroom – were in the nature of collisions. She was damaged....a minor scrape on a local street, a more serious prang on a country lane, a wreck on a two-lane carriageway, a smash-up on a major motorway, a head-on – potentially life-threatening – on a six-lane freeway. Each collision revealed the weaknesses in her structure. I want this – this idea, this reflection, this – retrospective to be in the nature of an exhibition in a gallery space, it's going to have to be a big one so we'll need the whole stage. Huge plinths will support these frozen installations – can you see it? What were once several moments of intense movement – two vehicles accidentally colliding, sometimes extremely violently – are now sculptures, static, still, stationary....viewers have all the time in the world to study the twisted metal, shattered glass and torn and bloodied interiors of the various vehicles involved.

— 193 —

TOMOS    What would you say to having them represented as holograms?

LANA     Holograms....yes, I like that.

TOMOS    It would add a sense of unreality.

LANA     Make it – dream-like.

TOMOS    You mean nightmarish.

LANA     N-i-g-h-t-m-a-r-i-s-h....what a beautiful word.

TOMOS    What about the music?

LANA     I'm very tired, you know. Tired of looking back.

TOMOS    Then stop.

LANA     Stop? Just like that? No, I can't.

TOMOS    You will.

LANA     ...Please tell me a little more about yourself...

TOMOS    Music first.

LANA     [*Frustrated exhale*] You choose.

TOMOS    Me? O-k-a-y....I think it's time for some *jazz*.

LANA     Wow. I don't know what I was expecting but I don't think I was expecting that. You're full of surprises.

TOMOS    You like that.

LANA     I do.

TOMOS    ...I would never trample on your silk sheets...

LANA    You wouldn't?

TOMOS   Never.

LANA    I like the idea of using jazz.

TOMOS   You like jazz, I know that from your writing.

LANA    The first LP I bought was a Louis Armstrong album.

TOMOS   I had something a bit different in mind – a bit more – umm – oh, *what's* the *word* I *want*...

*Pregnant pause*

LANA    Are you taking the piss?

TOMOS   What the hell does that mean!

LANA    Are you shaking my melons.

TOMOS   You mean am I making fun of you? [*Smiling*] Only slightly.

LANA    [*Tense*] If you start laughing at me – at my puny endeavours–

TOMOS   Avantgarde, that's the word I want. I wasn't laughing at you.

LANA    Because...

TOMOS   Your efforts are far from puny.

LANA    They are?

TOMOS   I wouldn't be here otherwise.Your work is completely worthy.

LANA    Honestly?

TOMOS   It's true. Don't ever doubt it.

— 196 —

LANA    That's....[*moved*]....that's one of the nicest things
        anyone has ever said to me. [*Recovering*] Better not
        say anything else if you want me to get any more
        work done today.

TOMOS   I know what I'm talking about. You haven't been
        encouraged enough. That's one of the biggest
        challenges of being an artist, the solitary struggle.

LANA    You know – if you ever manage to make me laugh
        at myself you will be breaking new ground.

TOMOS   Why don't we throw *all* that into the black hole?

LANA    We?

TOMOS   I'll help you.

LANA    But – I – how – I – what – I can't do that!

TOMOS   Okay, okay. Maybe it's too soon. Let's get back to
        the exhibition.

LANA    Exhibition?

TOMOS   The wrecked cars.

LANA    Yes, yes, let's get back to the wrecked cars. Any
        ideas?

TOMOS   One occurs to me. The other parties.

LANA    The other parties?

TOMOS   The other parties in the collisions.

LANA    What about them?

TOMOS   [*Lofty*] In a collision the damage is not restricted to one side alone.

LANA     Oh please, any form of preaching is strictly forbidden.

TOMOS   So you do remember some things. Touché.

LANA     Just the slights and insults. You're right though. You think I should describe the damage sustained by both sides then?

TOMOS   Yes.

LANA     You'll have to help me. Think you can do it?

TOMOS   That's what I'm here for. And I am uniquely qualified, am I not?

LANA     Being male.

TOMOS   Precisely. But you wanted me to choose the music, let's start with that.

# ACT SIX, SCENE THREE

TOMOS  Upbeat tempo or kind of slow?

LANA  Either – just so it's chaotic, demanding, not easy to listen to.

TOMOS  That doesn't surprise me. Well, it has to be Zorn then.

LANA  Zorrenn?

TOMOS  John Zorn, Z-o-r-n. Yep, he's your man.

LANA  Oh – Zawn. I don't think I've heard of him.

TOMOS  No? Seriously out there.

LANA  What does he play?

TOMOS  Tenor sax. I don't think you'll like his music. It's very – muscular, aggressive, definitely suitable.

LANA  And you think it will work?

TOMOS  Totally. Chaotic, demanding, not easy to listen to. Full of dissonance.

LANA  All right. I'll take your word for it.

TOMOS  Best of all, completely lacking in sentimentality.... so it will provide that sense of – of incongruity that you like to – uh – that you – uh – prefer to – that you seem to favour.

LANA  You were extremely careful there – in your choice of words.

— 199 —

TOMOS   [*Smiling*] I was.

[*They look at each other, there is a palpable flare of attraction.* LANA *looks away,* TOMOS *continues looking at her for a few more seconds*]

LANA    So – music settled. What next?

TOMOS   A procession of men – a sort of – echo – yes – an echo – of the procession of men you had parading across the stage in Act One. All those *types*.

LANA    The same men?

TOMOS   No. What we have here is the other parties in the collisions. The actual men involved.

LANA    Ah.

TOMOS   We observe them, looking around the exhibition in their various states of – of discomfort – no, that won't do. It has to be specific. They – they walk, limp, stumble, stagger – crawl, even – around the – the – what did you call them? Sculptures?

LANA    Frozen installations.

TOMOS   Okay, frozen installations. Depending on the seriousness of their injuries, they are – I mean he is, no, um, each man is – um – drawn – n-yah, not really – to the – the particular collision that indicates – no – um – shows – um, the representation – shit, no, that's horrible – I'm struggling here.

LANA    I know what you're trying to say. Each man gravitates to the species of collision in which he

— 200 —

received his injuries, the more serious the collision, the more gruesome the injuries.

TOMOS    Yes!

LANA    But then they *have* to be the same men – I mean a selection from that group – the ones who have slept with her.

TOMOS    No need to be so literal.

LANA    Don't confuse authenticity with catharsis, right?

TOMOS    Did I say that?

LANA    You did.

TOMOS    Well, it's true. Let's get back to the job in hand.

*END OF ACT SIX, SCENE THREE*

LANA    Tell me what really happens.

TOMOS   What?

LANA    The collisions, the sculptures, the wrecks – it's all
        metaphor. I'd like to hear the other side of things
        – the man's side. You said yourself the damage
        isn't restricted to just one side. Tell me about the
        men.

TOMOS   You already nailed it. That gap you described way
        back at the beginning – the gap in the male psyche
        that causes great pain. I think you called it a hole.

LANA    What about it?

TOMOS   It's at the root of the problem. And it's not
        confined to just some men, I'm pretty sure it's the
        case with all men. It's not a gap or a hole exactly.
        It's more a sense of – of lack, that something
        is lacking. Sometimes I think it's actually built
        in – into our biology, I mean. [*Bitter laugh*] And
        we spend half our lives trying to fill it. Hence the
        endless wrecks.

LANA    Is that how *all* men feel?

TOMOS   We're talking here about heterosexual men, right?

LANA    Right. And this – this – whatever we're calling it
        – this *la*–

TOMOS   –Every man has a hole in his soul that he is driven
        to fill.

LANA    His soul? You don't look like the religious sort.

— 202 —

TOMOS   I'm not. I mean his – his psyche.

LANA   And the best way to fill it is by – by –

TOMOS   By connecting with a woman, yeah. Well, there are other ways but most men are not interested in the amount of work involved in the alternatives, the spiritual route, I mean. So we look for a woman. Because we need to connect. And the lack of that connection causes physical pain – well, perhaps not physical but definitely psychical. Can you imagine that?

LANA   Of course. Who hasn't felt pain at some point in their life?

TOMOS   It's a very particular type of pain though – you appreciate irony, well here's the irony – the particular pain is unbearable because men are surrounded by what they regard as its potential remedy.

LANA   Meaning....women.

TOMOS   Right – and the big problem really is how to get your hands on one.

LANA   That's how you think of it – trying to get your hands on something that will stop the pain?

TOMOS   Depends on the man. But that's about the size of it, yeah.

LANA   Wow.

TOMOS   And believe me, it's not easy living with that amount of need.

— 203 —

LANA    I knew it, I knew it.

TOMOS   And that's before we even get into the issue of the
        other need – for power. The desire to be top dog.
        But we need to get back to the production. The
        audience is waiting for the next scene.

## ACT SIX, SCENE FOUR

LANA   Enid has no such sense of incompleteness when she is without a man. Intellectually she considers herself independent, an independent thinker, an independent doer. She can – and does – take care of herself, her own needs. She can function without a man. She does not trust the – the urge – the – the instinct – call it what you will – that impels her towards being part of a couple. Because for her the situation does not contain desire. The one thing that is not a feature of being with a man is desire. For her men are like machines and they have all been put together the same way.

TOMOS   Woah, that's pretty damning.

LANA   But isn't that exactly how men think of women?

TOMOS   No! I – look, let's get back to your story. What comes next?

LANA   We are going to have so much to talk about when this is over.

TOMOS   I agree, meanwhile, what comes next?

LANA   Enid takes the train to Washington DC, is patronised by her friends for a few days, then she flies back to London. Back to Bernard.

TOMOS   Then what?

LANA   She starts writing poetry.

TOMOS   Ah – The High Price Of Accommodation.

— 205 —

LANA      The Price of Accommodation.

TOMOS    I still think mine's a better title.

LANA      Well, that's neither here nor there because this
          poetry comes much earlier than that. This is the
          point at which Enid thinks she has found someone
          to whom she can give her love – of which there
          is an abundance. Deep deep down, in spite of
          everything, Enid still hopes. She has never learned
          to hate. Her potential for loving is still completely
          untapped, but she believes she has found an outlet.
          He has possessed her physically, now she will
          allow him to possess her....mm....what's the word
          I'm looking for.

TOMOS    Spiritually?

LANA      That'll do for now. Also, she is yearning for
          change, a complete change. She lives with Bernard
          but they have no sexual contact – Bernard loves
          her but she does not love him. They are both aware
          of this. For her, he is a friend – they are the best
          of friends. However, this is, understandably, not
          enough for Bernard therefore Bernard gets his –
          his satisfaction elsewhere. With Marvin, Enid has
          been made aware of her carnality – this is the gap
          that was waiting to be filled – but she is confusing
          it with love; his desire for her has swept her up
          into unknown territory and she thinks the desire is
          hers. She is calling this new terrain love, whereas
          in fact it is mere infatuation.

TOMOS    Sounds dangerous.

— 206 —

LANA        The stage is empty, bare of scenery, furniture, props. A sheet of paper flutters down from above the stage. After a few seconds, another sheet follows and then another and another, until the stage is alive with fluttering sheets of paper. Some of the sheets fall into the orchestra pit, causing great annoyance among the musicians, and some sheets fall into the audience. Those members of the audience who find themselves landed upon cannot help but take up the sheets of paper and attempt to read them, but the auditorium is too dark. Eventually the curiosity to know what is on the sheets of paper overcomes any sense of theatrical decorum and after a while, here and there, a match is lit, a lighter flicked on, a pocket flashlight utilised so that the words can be read. By now the stage is hip deep in accumulated sheets of paper and still they rain down, spilling over even further into the orchestra pit, forcing the musicians to stop playing – a sheet of paper caught in the bow of a cello or in the bell of a tuba does not make for music! The soundtrack grinds to a halt.

TOMOS       You haven't said what it was.

LANA        Mm?

TOMOS       You haven't described the music.

LANA        Oh....you do it.

TOMOS       *Me?*

LANA        Yes, you seem to have a good instinct for what works. You choose.

TOMOS    If you think so....o-k-a-y....why don't you tell me
what's written on the sheets of paper, that might
help – if I hear some of the words.

LANA    Do I have to?

TOMOS    It would be a help.

LANA    [*Exasperated sigh*] Very well. These are some of
the words written on the sheets of paper....if I
can stand to hear them....All right, here goes.
Ugh, [*shivers*]: *Life and Death are mumbo-jumbo,
Life is mumbo, Death is jumbo.* Hardly qualifies as
poetry but there it is. Okay, here's another: *A walk
down Railton Road in Brixton, south-west London, Is
like observing open-heart surgery, You know there's
something good and worthwhile going on, But you
can't bear to look because it's such a bloody mess.* I'm
rather fond of that one actually. Here's another:
*We lie together naked in the afternoon-warm room–*
Oh god, I can't, I just can't. It's too embarrassing.
To think that I – that Enid was such a little fool.

TOMOS    Don't be so hard on yourself. It's all in the past.

LANA    Easily said. So what do you think? Music-wise?

TOMOS    Streisand.

LANA    ...

TOMOS    Kidding. The Brixton poem inspired me. How
about some rap?

LANA    Perfect! I *love* rap!

*END OF ACT SIX, SCENE FOUR*

TOMOS   You love rap? That's a little difficult to believe.

LANA    I was joking. I hate rap.

TOMOS   You're worse than a seesaw! – or do you just enjoy it – this back and forth from one extreme to the next?

LANA    It's a curse I have to live with.

TOMOS   I see.

LANA    I have a better idea. Let's jump ahead, to the poem that sums it all up – the doomed relationship. This is the poem to keep in mind when you try to find the appropriate music. This one actually is from the anthology – that collection I mentioned ages ago, *The High Price of Accommodation*.

TOMOS   Good. Let's hear it.

LANA    [*Takes a breath*] *Every time I–*

TOMOS   Wait a minute, just a minute, you said, *The High Price of* – you've accepted my title?

LANA    Yes.

TOMOS   [*Thrilled*] W-o-w. And what's the poem about?

LANA    It's about – it's about a *woman's* need for connection, a *woman's* need for satisfaction. It's about Enid's endless naïvety, if that's the word – it's about her bamboo-like approach to relationships with men – correction – her relationship with this man. It's about endlessly thwarted desire.

TOMOS   Great. Fire away.

— 209 —

LANA      [*Takes a breath*] *Every time I fly out–*

TOMOS     –Wait.

LANA      Yes?

TOMOS     You said *bamboo-like*. That was a strange choice of words.

LANA      Listen to the poem, that will explain it.

TOMOS     Okay. Go ahead.

LANA      [*Takes a breath*] *Every time I fly out in hope–*

TOMOS     –Wait! Sorry to interrupt again. Does it have a title?

LANA      Yes, it has a title: *Nomansland*.

TOMOS     Okay, good. I promise I won't interrupt again.

LANA      [*Takes a deep breath*] Here goes: *Nomansland–*

TOMOS     –Wait! Sorry, sorry! But....shouldn't this be the next scene? A scene to itself? It's important, right?

LANA      Yes, it is. All right then, next scene.

TOMOS     I can see it. Can I – d'you mind? – if I tell you what I have in mind?

LANA      Please.

TOMOS     The piles and mounds of white paper are still all over the stage. A little girl comes in and picks up a single sheet then recites what's on that piece of–

LANA      [*Trancelike*] –Y-e-s....act six, scene five...

— 210 —

## ACT SIX, SCENE FIVE

LANA   ...the stage is still filled with the avalanche of
white paper. The orchestra plays in unison, very
softly, a sustained chord, minor key. A young girl
dressed in white – she is no more than thirteen –
enters, she picks her way carefully to downstage
centre – she has to step over piles of paper here
and there. She stops, turns, bends and selects a
single page from the mass then straightens. On
the page is a poem: she recites the first few lines.
A second woman enters, she is in her twenties,
she is also dressed in white. The young girl hands
the poem to the second woman who recites a few
more lines of the poem. A third woman enters,
she is in her thirties, dressed in white. The second
woman hands the poem to the third woman who
recites still more lines. A fourth woman enters, et
cetera...

And now comes a fifth woman. She recites the
whole poem.

*Nomansland*

*Every time I fly out in hope*
*Opening my wings gladly*
*Willingly*
*Trusting you to satisfy me*
*This time,*
*Giving myself like fruit upon a*
*Plate*
*I love you*

*I yearn to please you.*
*And that's what makes it*
*Hurt so much*
*When flying, high and hopefully, my*
*Happy willing wings outstretched,*
*You dash me to the ground*
*With your satisfaction.*

The fifth woman is left alone on stage. She turns and forces her way into the avalanche of white paper which soon envelopes her completely.

*END OF ACT SIX, SCENE FIVE*

TOMOS    You're better at this stuff than I am.

LANA    But you're the one who had the idea.

TOMOS    That's true.

*Pause*

TOMOS    I understand now....the bamboo....it's not naïvety,
it's optimism. She gets pushed down, beaten
down, but somehow she always manages to spring
back. It's optimism, isn't it?

LANA    You'd think she would have run out of it – after all
this time.

TOMOS    You were extremely patient back there – with my
interruptions.

LANA    I've decided it works sometimes, to let you guide
me.

TOMOS    I'm honoured. Okay, I have a suggestion – for a
different title – for the poem – for *Nomansland.*
Would you be open to that.

LANA    Try me.

*Pause*

TOMOS    *Hope.*

*Pause*

LANA    Nope.

TOMOS    Okay.

*Pause*

— 213 —

TOMOS   You used the word *love* – in the poem.

LANA    I know.

TOMOS   How could you have loved – him.

LANA    It was never really love. It was infatuation,
        madness, the need to escape, a desperation for
        change. After that, mostly pity – and then loyalty.
        And then, the fear of being abandoned, thinking
        I no longer knew how to live alone – how to be
        alone. And don't forget I was used to deprivation.
        He fed me crumbs, I was used to crumbs. A diet of
        crumbs.

TOMOS   Go on.

LANA    I read somewhere that the human brain can
        function for an hour on one peanut.

TOMOS   That sounds a bit far-fetched.

LANA    A hungry dog is an attentive dog.

TOMOS   What?

LANA    I don't want to talk about this any more. I'm ready
        to go on, to the next scene. It's the last one.

TOMOS   Fantastic!

LANA    I want my reward.

TOMOS   What d'you mean?

LANA    For never giving up, for trying so damned hard. I
        want to leapfrog over all the rest. I want to shovel
        it all into the black hole, all of it. I want to move

— 214 —

on. I want what you want. I WANT TO HAVE
DONE WITH IT.

TOMOS   Are you serious?

LANA   Deadly. I want it over, I want it finished. I want
what I deserve. New scene. I've no idea which it is.

TOMOS   Six. You're really going to do this?

# ACT SIX, SCENE SIX

LANA     Let's play leapfrog!

TOMOS   What?

LANA     Leapfrog!

TOMOS   Have you gone out of your mind?

LANA     The stage is a playground – in the background
         all the equipment usually associated with a kids'
         playground – swings, roundabout, climbing frame.
         in the foreground a couple of kids playing leapfrog
         – yes, leapfrog!

TOMOS   Oh, I see, okay, go ahead.

LANA     NO! – oh, how could I be so stupid! Clear the
         stage!! Clear the stage!!

TOMOS   You're not stupid. Erratic, yes, stupid, no.

LANA     The dancers! Bring on the dancers again!

TOMOS   You sure?

LANA     Just two dancers this time, in a pas de deux.

TOMOS   And what's that?

LANA     It's the bit of the ballet that everyone loves, the
         dance between the leading man and the leading
         lady, one of those exquisite Tchaikovsky ballet
         duets, say, that depict sex in a veiled manner. The
         male dancer is tall, muscular, very well endowed
         – there is no way to hide this fact since he is

— 216 —

required to wear such tight hose – while she is small, delicate, fragile, though stronger than she looks. Both have pleasing features and both have that superb control over their limbs and torsos that exemplifies a dancer in his or her prime. He lifts her effortlessly, she floats through the air with breathtaking ease and precision. He supports her as she bends and twists and arcs and turns. She leans into him, grateful for his tall muscular frame and his long dependable arms. Her need for him makes him feel important. His need for her makes her feel beautiful. They are the personification of male and female beauty, grace, agility and – what's the word I want – you know – that yin and yang thing where one complements the other? Complementariness.

TOMOS   Is that a word?

LANA   It is now. Yes, it's a word. A sadly neglected one, I might add.

TOMOS   Add away. Costumes?

LANA   Just as you'd expect.

TOMOS   I was sure you'd want to go in the opposite direction. Dress them in rags at the very least.

LANA   Hmmm. I don't want to become too predictable in my – contrariness.

TOMOS   Of course not. Conventional costumes then.

LANA   Yes. Let's have all the satin, silk, brocade, lace, sparkles, sequins and sprinkles we can get.

— 217 —

TOMOS    Why not.

LANA     However, while the performers dance, the
         audience is nervous, slightly agitated – they cannot
         help but feel apprehensive when recalling the
         involuntary stabs of horror and dismay they have
         been made to experience in the midst of every
         earlier encounter in this production between
         the male and the female. The pattern has been
         clearly established and they have been conditioned
         to expect it. We have achieved a disagreeable
         dysequilibrium in their outlook.

TOMOS    Exactly what you set out to do – kill off their
         appetite for romance. No more happy ever after!

LANA     Y-e-s....they dislike this simmering sense of dread.
         And added to this – this – uh – in addition to
         feeling this incipient dread, they also note that the
         stage is littered with obstacles, obstacles that have
         to be negotiated by the dancing couple. How will
         the dancers continue performing their graceful
         pas de deux when they are surrounded by these
         obstacles? To put it colloquially, they think: *Here
         we go again.*

TOMOS    What are the obstacles?

LANA     They dance towards one of the obstacles, but a
         split second before the moment of impact, with a
         muffled, explosive sound, the obstacle implodes,
         collapses, falls in a shapeless insignificant heap
         at the dancers' feet. All hindrance gone, the
         male dancer lifts the female dancer – she seems
         to be featherlight – over the top of the small

— 218 —

insignificant heap at their feet and, their gorgeous costumes intact and unsullied, they continue their marvellous duet.

TOMOS    But what are the obstacles?!

LANA     Balloons.

TOMOS    Balloons! That's ludicrous! Oh no, this time you've really gone too far.

*END OF ACT SIX, SCENE SIX*

LANA    But don't you see? It's the perfect way to depict
them – the monsters of the past – and the fact that
I've accepted it all now. I've reduced the monsters
to – to – nonentities. I've defeated them – their
hold over me. It's all – history!

TOMOS   Great! But the balloons – you're gonna have to
describe them – to me, if not to the audience.

LANA    Of course I am going to describe them. That's easy.
They are those grotesque balloons that you see
dancing and flopping around outside car washes
and car dealerships – they look like tall tethered
skinny ghosts with ragged hair and – just for a
second – when air is pumped into them and they
spring up and lurch and bend and their thin arms
start waving around – just for a second, they are
terrifying and then in the next second you see
them for what they are and they're ridiculous and
then you – you can't help laughing at yourself for
being so scared for that one second but you forgive
yourself and you even despise them a little because
you're embarrassed, you don't quite know what to
do with that moment of fear, because it was caused
by a – a long skinny balloon full of air! And then
you move on....you move on. Until the next time.

TOMOS   So will they keep popping up? While the dancers
are on stage?

LANA    Oh yes, let's do that, I'd love that.

## ACT SIX, SCENE SEVEN

LANA    The exquisite pas de deux goes on and the silly
balloon monsters spring up and collapse and spring
up again, and the dancers just carry on. Sometimes
the monsters are part of the dance, they pop up
between the dancers' legs, they butt in between the
man and the woman, making the audience laugh,
because the obstacles are a known quantity now
but what's important – what's important is....no-
one can predict where or when they will pop up
next, it's random, unpredictable, so now the whole
thing is a kind of game, now it's humorous, the
anticipation, the slight shock – the randomness.
Lights to black.

*END OF ACT SIX, SCENE SEVEN*

LANA    Well, I think that's about it.

TOMOS   –I love you.

LANA    I know.

TOMOS   I want to make you happy.

LANA    I know.

TOMOS   I have to tell you though, I'm a bit nervous.

LANA    You are?

TOMOS   It's been a while since I – since I was with a woman. Any woman.

LANA    What are you afraid of?

TOMOS   I'm not afraid, just – a little nervous.

LANA    It's been a while since I was with a man.

TOMOS   But I'm not going to let nervousness stop me from doing what I want to do.

*Pause*

LANA    [*Earnest*] So tell me all about yourself now – about your earlier life, your marriage, where you were born, all that stuff. I think it's about time, don't you? Tell me *everything* about yourself.

TOMOS   Woh! – maybe you'd like me to do a couple of back somersaults while I'm at it? Okay, I was married for almost twenty years – she left me for another man.

LANA    Ah.

TOMOS   Yes, ah. You have no idea how many times I said that – *Ah*.

LANA    But....you said you were a widower!

TOMOS   Delaying tactics.

LANA    What do you mean?

TOMOS   Well....it's not exactly the finest moment in a man's life, is it? – admitting that his wife left him after twenty years. I had every intention of telling you but I didn't – I didn't have the nerve.

LANA    But that wouldn't have put me off. It doesn't put me off.

TOMOS   No?

LANA    No. In fact, let's throw that into the black hole too.

TOMOS   I think it's already *in* there! Okay, here's some of what you want to know: I'm a year younger than you, I'm a Taurus. I was born in Columbus Ohio but I grew up in Chicago, I went to university there, as an English major, and ended up teaching. I did a lot of travelling, mostly in the east. I got married when I was twenty-five, divorced when I was forty-four, my ex-wife lives somewhere in South America. We had twin girls, one died in a car crash when she was nineteen, the other now lives in Australia, we have very little contact. I live here in the same city you do, about fifteen minutes drive from the centre, I don't smoke but I do drink – not as much as I used to, I have a brother and a

— 223 —

sister – I usually see them a couple of times a year. My father died ten years ago, my mother died last year. And for breakfast – since that was part of the questionnaire – I usually have coffee and toast for breakfast.

LANA  That's what I have for breakfast.

TOMOS  And....I'd like to tell you about the book I'm reading right now.

LANA  A book? Certainly.

TOMOS  I'm reading a book called *She Comes First* which tells men how to make love to a woman so *she'll* have a good time.

LANA  [*Incredulous*] Non-fiction?

TOMOS  Mm-hmm. Can't recall the author. You can look it up if you like.

LANA  What's the title again?

TOMOS  *She Comes First.*

LANA  Meaning....in bed.

TOMOS  Yes. I want to be – educated.

LANA  And is it working?

TOMOS  I haven't had a chance to – well, let's say, I've yet to find out. The opportunity hasn't–

LANA  You know, when you were introduced to me, at the Meet and Greet party, something flared up inside me.

TOMOS    Flared up?

LANA     It was like a spark being ignited. A tiny flame.

TOMOS    Yeah?

LANA     I'd never felt anything like it before. It was – well, the Japanese have an expression – koi no yokan.

TOMOS    Say that again.

LANA     Koi no yokan.

TOMOS    And what does it mean exactly?

LANA     A premonition of love. That's what I felt.

TOMOS    Coino yokun. And you believe in it – in that kind of thing?

LANA     You don't have to believe it – you just have to experience it and recognise it. The feeling comes first, the label comes later. And it's undeniable. So I can't tell you how difficult it has been, how awful it's been, revealing all these gruesome details about – about...

TOMOS    Your past.

LANA     Yes.

TOMOS    Which is over.

LANA     Yes.

TOMOS    I felt it too.

LANA     What, a premonition?

— 225 —

TOMOS   It was more of a physical pull – a very strong
        physical attraction.

LANA    You fancied me.

TOMOS   Oh yes, but it went much deeper than that – I
        thought, this woman is the part of me that's been
        missing.

LANA    Oh....the usual then.

TOMOS   Ouch.

LANA    You know....I got it wrong....the black hole – I
        was using it all wrong – the black hole doesn't
        represent the human appetite for romance. What
        it represents is – life. Life! The whole ghastly,
        glorious, messy business of being alive: the bitter,
        the sweet, the flowers, the failures, all of it!....
        the [*emphatic*] badly decorated, sharp-cornered,
        poorly lit, endlessly tedious, yet infuriatingly
        unpredictable, [*slower*] excruciatingly precious
        prison we rumble around in.

TOMOS   Careful with those adverbs.

LANA    It's – it's almost unbearable.

TOMOS   I see that.

*Pause*

TOMOS   Lana.

LANA    Yes?

TOMOS   Give me your hand.

— 226 —

*[LANA holds out her hand and he takes it, kisses it very gently then releases it]*

LANA   One final scene. There is one last scene.

TOMOS   Go ahead.

## ACT SIX, SCENE EIGHT

LANA     The stage is completely bare. Slowly, everyone in
the production – every single actor – from the
smallest and the youngest, to the largest, oldest
– walks alone onto the stage. It is a slow process
because there are so many of them – hundreds
of them and they have to stand closer and closer
together. There is no hierarchy of appearance,
no yielding of centre stage to a bigger star, they
all simply squeeze together, in one mass, more
and more tightly, until the stage is crammed with
bodies. There is no jostling. The audience is caught
unawares, thinking this is just another scene and
not the final one. There is a slight disturbance in
the midst of the crowd and one actor is pushed
forward to the front – it is Enid – then another – it
is Marvin. They stand very far apart on opposite
sides of the stage. Enid faces front, Marvin looks
over at her, she continues to face out, ignoring
him. All eyes in the gathered mass of people
are wide open, watching, but otherwise there
is complete stillness and silence. Still looking at
Enid, Marvin opens his mouth to say something,
doesn't, turns and melts back into the mass of
bodies. Enid gives a loud, pronounced exhalation
of relief. Another slight disturbance simmers deep
within the mass of bodies, expands, is followed by
a wave of movement, and a tall man is urged to the
front of the crowd. It is Tomos.

*CURTAIN*

Made in the USA
Las Vegas, NV
17 January 2024

84428376R00142